序　言

很多人一想到要寫英文信，就害怕。有了這本書，就很方便了。只要按照本書內容，抄一抄、改一改就行了。抄多了，自己自然就會寫，原來，寫英文書信並不可怕。

英文書信和中文不同，有固定的格式，我們特別將各種信封、各種信紙，不同的寫法，一一列出。讀者要學寫英文信，就要先從學信封和信紙的格式開始。

「萬用書信英文」的內容非常齊全，只要你想得到的內容，書中都有，從一般問候到寫情書，從申請入學到請病假，從求職信到辭職信，樣樣齊全，等於英文書信的寶典，人人需要。你想要寫什麼英文書信，可先查看本書的目錄，目錄就是索引。

由於FAX、E-mail的到來，英文書信更為重要。這本書非常適合當教科書，讓學生背、讓學生練習寫英文書信，學生會很有成就感，覺得所學的，立刻可以用得到，很多學校採用本書後，學生非常喜歡上英文課。會寫英文書信，一生受用無窮。

本書原為史濟蘭老師編著，書名原為「現代書信英文」，這次經過美籍老師 Laura E. Stewart 重新修訂，編者重新更新內容，更符合現代讀者的需要。

本書雖經多次審慎的校對，疏漏之處恐在所難免，誠盼各界先進不吝指正。

編者　謹識

目　　錄

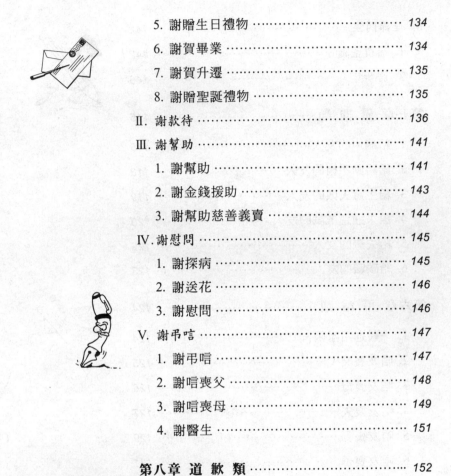

第九章 情 書 類 ·················· 166

第十一章 學 校 類 …………………… 233

第一篇　英文書信的格式

BY AIR MAIL
PAR AVION

第一章 英文信封的寫法

　　書寫信封應達到三個要點，即正確、易讀及美觀。

1. 郵票應貼在（信封）正面右上角。
2. 寄信人姓名、地址寫在正面左上角。
3. 收信人姓名、地址寫在正面的中央或右下四分之一處（見附圖）。

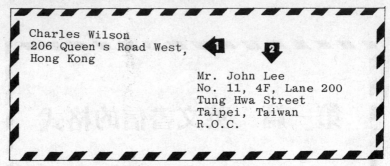

　　　　　1 寄信人姓名、地址

　　　　　2 收信人姓名、地址

也有人將寄信人姓名、地址寫在信封背後，收信人姓名地址寫在信封正面的中央。

I. 郵票的位置

當郵票的張數不只一張時，先考慮由右往左，然後再往下。

II. 寄信人、收信人姓名、地址寫法

1. 鋸齒式（Indented Style）

為英國傳統的格式，每往下一行，就縮進去一、兩個字母而成鋸齒狀。現在已很少人用。

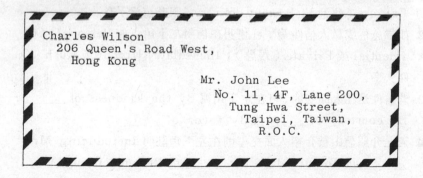

```
Charles Wilson
  206 Queen's Road West,
    Hong Kong

                    Mr. John Lee
                  No. 11, 4F, Lane 200,
                    Tung Hwa Street,
                      Taipei, Taiwan,
                        R.O.C.
```

2. 齊頭式（Block Style）

為美國式用法，每一行齊頭並列（參照 p.2 ）。是最常用的格式。

3. 折衷式（Semi - block　Style）

```
Charles Wilson
206 Queen's Road West,
Hong Kong

                    Mr. John Lee
                      No. 11, 4F, Lane 200,
                        Tung Hwa Street,
                          Taipei, Taiwan,
                            R.O.C.
```

Ⅲ. 信封上的其他指示

1. 信件的性質，可註明於信封明顯處，如 Registered（掛號），By air mail, Par Avion（航空信），Printed matter（印刷品），Express（快遞），Prompt delivery（限時專送）等。

2. 如為急件或私人信件等，可註明在信封左下角，如 Personal, Confidential 或 Private（親啓）；Immediate, Urgent 或 Rush（急件）等。

3. 若信件是託人面交的，可在左下角寫 By the kindness of _____, By courtesy of _____ 或 By favor of _____。

4. 若是介紹信由被介紹人面交，則在左下角註明 Introducing Mr. _____ 或 To introduce Mr. _____ 或 Recommending Mr. _____。

5. 若信件是要寄給A，但請B轉交，則先寫A再寫B，並在B之前加 c/o（care of 由…轉交）。

第二章　英文信的格式

I.格　式

　　英文信的格式，也包括鋸齒式（Idented Style）, 齊頭式（Block Style）和折衷式（Semi-block Style）。

20 Po Ai Road,
Taipei, Taiwan,
Republic of China
15th December, 2003

Dear Sabrina,

　　Thank you for your invitation to the party on 20th December. *I would like to be able to come, but I am afraid that I have been invited to visit friends in Macau on that day* and so I am afraid that I shall not be able to accept your invitation.

　　I wish I could lend you my tape recorder, but I am afraid that it is being mended at the moment and it will not be returned to me until after your party. I am very sorry about this, but I hope you can borrow one from *someone else*.

　　I am sure that you will have a very good party and wish I could be there.

With love,

....

鋸齒式（日期的各行及本文各段皆右縮數格）

35 Park Street
Tainan, Taiwan
Republic of China
November 29, 2003

Dear William,

I am delighted to hear of your recent marriage and now send you and your wife my warmest congratulations and best wishes for a very happy married life together.

I hope that when you have settled down in your new home you will bring your wife to see me, for I look forward very much to meeting her.

I am sending you a small present with this letter and I hope you and your wife will find it of some use.

With my best wishes to you both,

Yours sincerely,

....

齊頭式（各段左側皆對齊，不右縮）

25 Ching Tao E. Road
Taipei, Taiwan
Republic of China
June 11, 2003

Dear Julia,

Tom and I regret so very much that we will not be able to attend Margaret's wedding on Wednesday, June the seventeenth.

It was so thoughtful of you to ask us, but our tour around the island starts on June the seventh and we will not be back in time for the wedding.

We send our very best wishes to Carolyn and Steve, and we shall be with them in spirit on the happy day.

Fondly,

....

折衷式（住址及謙稱、簽名等爲齊頭式，信文爲鋸齒式）

* 鋸齒式多在發信人、收信人姓名、地址、日期等末端加標點符號（如p.5），稱爲閉塞式（Closed punctuation），是英國傳統用法，已漸少用。

而齊頭式則不在末端加標點符號（如p.6），稱爲開放式（Open punctuation）是美式用法。現在則以混合式（Mixed punctuation）最爲常用，即除了稱呼之後用冒號或逗號，結尾謙稱用逗號以外，其餘則不用標點。

Ⅱ.英文信結構

英文書信包含六個部分，即

    1. 寄信人地址及日期（ The Heading ）

    2. 收信人姓名及地址（ Inside Address ）

    3. 稱呼（ The Salutation ）

    4. 信文（內容）（ The Body ）

    5. 結尾謙稱（ The Complimentary Close ）

    6. 簽名（ The Signature ）

1. 寄信人地址及日期（ The Heading ）

寄信人地址，用以表明信的來處。日期則表明寫信的時間。但是大部分的機關、公司、行號的專用信紙，都有印妥的名稱地址（見 p.9），這種情形下只須再加上日期即可。

(1) 位置：在信紙的右上方。爲美觀起見，在信紙頂端與地址之間應留
       出一點空間。

(2) 在此部分不可寫上寄信人姓名。

(3) 地址的寫法是由小地方而大地方。日期寫在地址之下。

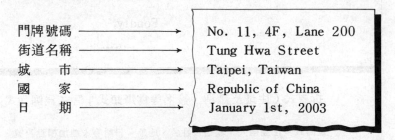

門牌號碼   ⟶   No. 11, 4F, Lane 200

街道名稱   ⟶   Tung Hwa Street

城   市   ⟶   Taipei, Taiwan

國   家   ⟶   Republic of China

日   期   ⟶   January 1st, 2003

(4) 日期的寫法，在英國較常用的是按日、月、年的順序，如：

           12th October, 2003

           3rd May, 2003

           5th June, 2003

美國人習慣上則以月、日、年為日期之順序，如：

> November 6, 2003
>
> May 5, 2003
>
> 11 / 6 / 2003

因英美日月順序相反，為避免造成誤解，11 / 6 / 2003 的寫法宜少用。此外在正式的書信中，月份名稱應該完整的寫出來，不宜縮寫。

(5)地址日期的排列，現在常用的是齊頭並列的方式（參照 p.8）。也有人用次行比前行縮進一兩個字母的方式。

> 101 Trumpington Road,
>
> Cambridge,
>
> England.
>
> > 3rd July, 2003

2. 收信人姓名、地址（Inside Address）

(1)一般社交信可省略此部分，但在商業信函的正式格式中，必須把收信人的姓名及地址寫在信紙的第一頁上，位置就在信紙左邊，約在日期下兩、三行。

> BORNEO COMPANY LTD
>
> 326 SILOM ROAD
>
> BANGKOK THAILAND
>
> > Cables: 'Borneo Bangkok'
> >
> > 4th February, 2003
>
> Mr. John J. Wiley
>
> Ajax Oil Company
>
> 246 Broadway
>
> Oklahoma City 5, OK

(2) 已知對方的頭銜時，應稱呼其正式頭銜，如 Dr. W. Johnson, Prof. E. Wright, the Personnel Manager ，而不用 Mr. 來稱呼他。

(3) 寄往外國的信，為避免送錯，應寫出所投遞國家的名稱。同樣的道理，信寄往美國時，除了要寫出國名外，在城市的名字後面，要加上州名，如：

> General Manager
> Berneo Company Inc.
> 100 Lakeside Drive
> Pacific Beach, Maryland
> U.S.A. ◀2 ⬆1

1. 州名
2. 國名

(4) 信件所投遞的地區，若有郵遞區號（ zip code ）應加上，以便迅速傳遞。郵遞區號的位置在州名或都市名之後（見附圖）。

> Mr. George Jones
> Vice President
> All American Toys Inc.
> 326 Van Ness
> San Francisco, CA 90123 ◀
> U.S.A.

1. 郵遞區號

3. 稱呼（ The Salutation ）

(1) 商業書信中，最常用的稱呼是 Dear Sir：稱呼之後須用冒號。如對方為合夥公司，則用複數形的 Dear Sirs：美式用法則多以 Gentlemen：來代替 Dear Sirs：。

(2) 一般的社交信，則要以關係的深淺，而用不同的稱呼。但稱呼之後要用逗點。

① 寫給不認識的人，可用

　　　　　Dear Sir,

② 寫給認識或僅知其姓名的人，可用

　　　　　Dear Mr. A,

　　　　　Dear Mrs. A,（已婚女姓）

　　　　　Dear Miss A,（單身女姓）

　　　　　Dear Ms. A,（已婚或單身女姓）

　　　Mr. R.C. Tsui

　　　General Manager

　　　Kowloon Express Dry Cleaners

　　　P.O. Box 6023

　　　Kowloon, Hong Kong

1　　Dear Mr. Tsui,

1. 稱呼

③ 寫給熟識的人，如親屬、好友，可用

　　　　　Dear Mother,

　　　　　Dear Uncle,

　　　　　Dear Granny,

④ 寫給親密的人，如丈夫、妻子、情人，可用

　　　　　Dearest David,

　　　　　Darling Vanya,

4. 信文（The Body）

信文即信的內容，全信最重要的部分。

(1)開始寫之前應該想清楚要寫些什麼。

(2)信文的位置在稱呼的下面一行或兩行處開始寫。

(3)信文要簡明、易讀，語氣要自然誠懇。

(4)若有結尾祝福語，要在信文最後另寫一行。

Dear Thomas,

I am delighted to hear of your promotion to Assistant Manager in the Sales Department. Very many congratulations! All of us who have seen you at work know that you owe your promotion to the hard work you have done for the last five years. You must be very proud of yourself and I think that you have every reason to be.

I am sure that you will find your new work enjoyable and exciting and I look forward to hearing of your next success.

1 With many congratulations and my best wishes for the future,

2 Yours sincerely,
Tom Liu

1 結尾祝福語 2 結尾謙稱

5. 結尾謙稱（The Complimentary Close）

(1) 位置

① 在鋸齒式書信中，結尾謙稱寫在信文下面中間偏右地方。

② 在齊頭式書信中，結尾謙稱則與信文齊頭。

③ 在折衷式書信中，結尾謙稱也是寫在信文下面中間偏右地方。

(2) 開頭第一個字母要大寫，後面須有逗點。

⑶結尾謙稱須與稱呼相配合，因爲結尾謙稱也因關係的深淺而有不同。下面是最常見的用法：

① Sincerely 在美式書信中最常見，其次是 Yours sincerely，可用於各種書信，尤其是商業函件。

② Respectfully yours 和 Yours respectfully 用於地位或輩份比自己高的人。

③ Yours truly 和 Very truly yours 用於不大熟悉的人。

④ As always 和 As ever 用於親屬及好友。

⑤ Love 和 With love, Lots of love 用於情侶、夫妻和女性密友。

6. 簽名（Signature）

⑴位置：在結尾謙稱的下面。

⑵務必要親筆簽名，如用打字，仍須在其上方親筆簽名。

⑶除非寫給熟悉或親密的人，簽名必須簽上姓和名，而且要使人能看得清楚。

⑷簽名不可附帶頭銜，如 Mr. John Smith。只須簽上自己的姓名如 John Smith。但是女性在寫信給不認識的人時，爲表明自己已婚或未婚，可簽：

（Miss）Rita Wright

或（Mrs. Robert）Rita Wright

如用打字，則可不加括弧，但仍須在其上方親筆簽名。

1. 親筆簽名

1. 親筆簽名

　　除了以上六個主要部分，有時在信寫好後，覺得還有話要說，或在本文中漏寫了，或寫完本文以後才發生的事情，要加以追述，便可以在簽名下一行，信紙左邊加 P.S.（Postscript）寫起，如爲重大事情，則在其後填入本人名字的字首。

　　如在一開始，就計劃性地做 P.S. 處理也許有效果，但不宜濫用。

＜正式英文書信的格式＞

No. 11, 4F, Lane 200
Tung Hwa Street
Taipei, Taiwan
R.O.C.
January 2, 2003

Mr. Thomas Evans
34 Mocon Street
New York, NY 11216
U.S.A.

Dear Mr. Evans,

Yours sincerely,

Philip Wang

P.S.

第二篇　社交信範文

第一章　通知類

Ⅰ.各項通知

1. 結婚通知

　　正式的結婚通知是雕版精印的，婚禮前用來送給沒有被邀請觀禮或參加婚宴的雙方友人。

　　新居地址可以印在結婚通知的左下角。

After the first of December

25 Elm Street, Creattown

　　也可以印成新居地址卡，附在結婚通知裏，一併寄出。(參閱P.32)

正式的結婚通知

Mr. and Mrs. Tem Po Wu

have the honour of announcing

the marriage of their daughter

Aileen

to

Mr. John Wang

on Saturday, the fifth of December

Holy Family Catholic Church

Taipei

＊ 吳天寶夫婦謹通知，他們的女兒愛琳與王約翰先生，將於十二月五日星期六，在台北天主教聖家堂舉行婚禮。

若因病或其他原因，取消婚禮，則用下式通知。

正式的婚禮取消通知

Mr. and Mrs. Tem Po Wu

announce that the marriage of their daughter

Aileen

to

Mr. John Wang

will not take place

* 吳天寶夫婦謹通知，他們的女兒愛琳與王約翰先生的婚禮將不舉行。

2. 通知訂婚

通知訂婚

March 2, 2003

My dearest Father,

　　I have a piece of news to tell you which I
think will surprise you very much. I have accepted Jack's proposal！ He came over yesterday
and asked me to be his wife. We have been in love
with each other for a long time. I know that all my
happiness lies in his hands, and all his happiness
in mine. I do hope, dear Father, that you will
approve of what I have done. If I could only
tell you what it means to us, I am certain you
would be glad. Do let me hear from you as soon
as possible.

　　　　　　　　Your affectionate daughter,

　　　　　　　　....................

通知訂婚 (二)

February 28, 2003

Dear Father,

    I'm going to surprise you very much — I'm engaged to be married to Helen Wang. We arranged it last night. I am feeling so happy I hardly know what I am doing. I do hope you will approve of the step I am taking. As you are aware, I am now making a fair income with every prospect of advancement, and I am sure I shall be ever so much happier married than I am at present. I have known Helen for about four years. She is the best and dearest girl in the world, very sensible, a good housekeeper, and universally popular. I want you very much to see more of her, and get to like her more and more. She has always liked you, and one of the first things she said after accepting my proposal was " I do so hope your father will care for me."

        Your affectionate son,

        ....

---

* I do hope you will approve of the step I am taking. … and I am sure I shall be ever so much happier married than I am at present. 希望您會同意我這樣做。您知道我現在已有相當的收入，升遷的希望也很大，我相信結婚後，我將會比現在更加快樂。

通知訂婚㈢

April 19, 2003

Dear Jack,

At college you used to say I was a lucky fellow. You were right！ I've found the most wonderful girl, and she's promised to marry me. Her name is Jenny Hsia and she lives in Kao-hsiung.

I am anxious to have you two meet, and I hope we can arrange it soon.

Fondly,

....

3. 通知嬰兒誕生

嬰兒誕生報喜的方式很多，最漂亮大方的是用一張小小的卡片，印上嬰兒的名字和出生日期，用一段白色或粉紅色的絲帶繫在父母兩人用的名片上，由父母分寄親友。如下例

Robert Wang, Jr.

July tenth

Mr. and Mrs. Robert Wang

47 Pace Place

下面這一封信是嬰兒的祖父母（或外祖父母）向他們的朋友報喜所寫的。

告知嬰兒誕生

（Date）

Dear Alice and Harry,

    The darlingest little fellow arrived last Thursday, June 16th. He has downy black hair, large eyes, looks like Jim, and has vocal chords which command effective attention when he wants something. He is a healthy, sturdy youngster. His mother, too, is well, and as you see, is wasting no time telling our dear friends how happy the parents are with their new son. And his proud father entertains not the slightest doubt that his radiant offspring will become a great man.

                Sincerely yours,

               …………………

*   上星期四，即六月十六日，可愛的小傢伙誕生了。他有著柔軟的黑頭髮，大大的黑眼睛，長得像吉姆。需要什麼時，他的聲帶會有效地引起他人注意。他是個健壯的小傢伙。他的母親也很好，如你們所想像的一樣，她正迫不及待，要朋友們分享添丁的喜悅。而他得意的父親則深信他的兒子將成爲偉人。

* sturdy〔'stɝdɪ〕*adj*. 健壯的

* entertain〔,ɛntɚ'ten〕*vt*. 懷抱（希望）

* radiant〔'redɪənt〕*adj*. 明亮的；燦爛奪目的

* offspring〔'ɔf,sprɪŋ〕*n*. 後代

4. 死亡通知

死亡的消息應立即通知近親好友，用電話或電報都可以，有時則寫信通知。

告知死訊

(Date)

Dear Carolyn,

We don't know why these things happen but happen they do. I have distressing news concerning your nephew, Jimmie Jackson. Jimmie died in an airplane crash on his way to Paris. I don't have many details, but there is one thing we know— death came instantly.

To you and to me and to those who were privileged to know Jimmie, his warm smile, his light heart, and his ready and infectious wit will always be among our fondest memories. Every hour spent in his company was a happy, joyous time which we can cherish.

I share your sorrow in this great loss.

Sincerely,

....

* airplane crash 飛機墜毀；空難
* infectious 〔 ɪn'fɛkʃəs 〕 *adj.* 有傳染性的
* cherish 〔 'tʃɛrɪʃ 〕 *vt.* 珍視

告知死訊㈡

(Date)

Dear Aunt,

As you know, dear Uncle Tom was in failing health for a long time. He died last night as he lived, clam, composed, quiet to the end. Everything possible was done for Uncle Tom but to no avail.

You are too far away to come for the funeral. We have no plans for Aunt Sarah as yet. If you have any suggestions, we would appreciate them. She is bearing up bravely. We will be in touch with you soon after the funeral.

Affectionately,

....

* to no avail 無效
* As you know, … Everything possible was done for Uncle but to no avail. 如你所知的，長久以來湯姆叔叔的健康情形就每下愈況。昨晚他過世了，平靜、安祥，如生前一樣。所有能爲他做的我們都做了，無奈徒勞無功。

告知死訊㈢

（Date）

Dear Mr. Wu,

　　I am writing to let you know that my father, Sidney B. Balister, died on Thursday, June the fourth, after a short illness.

　　He had mentioned you as a friend so often that I knew you would want to be informed.

　　　　　　　　　　　　Sincerely,

　　　　　　　　　　　　………

---

* He had mentioned you as a friend so often that I knew you you would want to be informed. 他常常提及您這位朋友，因此我知道您希望獲知這個消息。

告知死訊 ㈣

（Date）

Dear Miss Huang,

　　I am sorry to write you that my husband, Richard Meyer, passed away this Tuesday, the twenty-seventh of April.

　　I know that you and he have been good friends since college, and that you would want to be informed.

　　　　　　　　　　　　Sincerely yours,

　　　　　　　　　　　　………

告知死訊㈤

(Date)

Dear Uncle Ted,

Something has happened that was a great shock to us and I am afraid will be to you as well. Mother, who, as you know, had been ill for some years, passed away last night in her sleep.

The funeral is to be held at St. Anastasia Church on Forest Avenue, Janesville, Tuesday at three o'clock. Burial will be at Fairlawn Cemetery.

We know you join in our prayers and in our sorrow.

Affectionately,

．．．．．．．．．．．．

* avenue〔'ævəˌnju〕 *n.* 大街
* cemetery〔'sɛməˌtɛrɪ〕 *n.* 墓地

5. 通知購買新居

通知購買新居

（Date）

Dear Helen,

　　At last my dream has come true. I know you will be glad to learn that we have bought a house, for you know how much I've wanted this to happen. We're very happy. We have a small vegetable garden. Each of the children has claimed a little square of it, and I can see now that even if we have nothing else to eat, we'll have plenty of radishes.

　　How I wish that you could come and visit! If there's any possibility, do make every effort. We can make you comfortable, and it would be a joy to have you with us.

　　I've always told you about my problems, and I wanted you to share my happiness, too.

　　　　　　　　　Affectionately,

　　　　　　　　　…………

* claim〔klem〕*vt.* 請求
* radish〔'rædɪʃ〕*n.* 紅蘿蔔
* I've always told you about my problems, and I wanted you to share my happiness too. 我總是讓你分擔我的煩惱，因此希望你也能分享我的快樂。

6. 通知遷居

通知遷居

（Date）

Dear Robert,

I just moved two weeks ago. My new address is:

No. 3, Second Floor, Lane 198,
Chien-Kuo North Road
Taipei 231
TAIWAN ROC

Sincerely,
....

7. 通知派送物品

通知送貨到新家

（Date）

Dear Sir,

I am moving with my family to your neigh-
bourhood on January lst, and shall be grateful if you
will arrange to deliver bread, milk and other dairy
products as of that date.

Our new address will be:

No. 11, 4F, Lane 200,
Tung Hwa Street,
Taipei,
Thanks.

Yours truly,
....

8. 通知改換地址

通知變更地址

（Date）

Gentlemen :

Please change my address on your subscription rolls from:

No. 1, 4F, Alley 14

Lane 186, Tung Hwa Street, Taipei

to

No. 11, 4F, Lane 200,

Tung Hwa Street, Taipei

Thank you.

Very truly yours,

．．．．．．．．．．．．．．．．．．．

---

* subscription rolls 訂閱名冊

* Please … Tung Hwa Street, Taipei 請將我在你們的訂戶名冊上的
地址改變，從台北市通化街 186 巷 14 弄 1 號 4 樓

　　改爲

台北市通化街 200 巷 11 號 4 樓

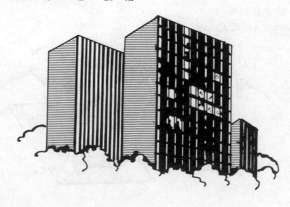

9. 通知不能赴約

取消約會通知

（Date）

Dear Mr. Wu,

    I greatly regret that owing to a sudden business call to Singapore next week, I shall be unable to keep my appointment fixed for next Tuesday morning. I will telephone you on my return to Taipei in order to make another appointment.

    I hope this cancellation will not cause you undue inconvenience.

    My best regards.

Yours sincerely,

....

*　　非常抱歉，因突然接獲通知，下星期須前往新加坡處理商務，以致未能往赴原定下星期二上午的約會。我回台北之後將與你通電話，再定會面日期。

我希望，取消這項約會，不致使你太過不便。

謹此問候。

* undue〔ʌn'dju〕*adj.* 過分的

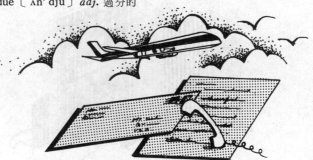

Ⅱ.公開啓事

喜喪事除分別函告親友之外，也有在報上刊登啟事的，茲各舉一例：

誕生啓事

Mr. and Mrs. Bunsen Wang of 1 Yu Nung Rd, Tainan, announce the birth of a son, John Wang, in Provincial Tainan Hospital on Sunday, October 17.

---

* 王本生夫婦，住台南市裕農路 1 號謹通知，其子王約翰，於十月十七日星期日，於省立台南醫院出生。

訂婚啓事

Delon — Acker. The engagement is announced of C.P. Delon, eldest son of Mr. and Mrs. D.S. Delon, Singapore, to Margaret Acker, eldest daughter of Mr. and Mrs. B.W. Acker of Garden city, America.

---

* 狄龍與艾嘉訂婚啓事——新加坡 D.S. 狄龍夫婦的長子 C.P. 狄龍，與美國花園市 B.W. 艾嘉夫婦的長女瑪格麗特艾嘉，宣告訂婚。

結婚啓事

Mr. and Mrs. Bunsen Wang of South-East street, Hsin-Chu City announce the marriage of their daughter Eileen Wang to Clay Roth, son of Mr. and Mrs. Alexander Roth of Kensington, at St. Anne's Church, Greenville.

* 王本生夫婦，住新竹市東南街，謹通知，他們的女兒王愛琳與京士頓城亞力山大洛士夫婦之子克雷洛士，在格連威爾的聖安尼教堂結婚。

訃 告

Tom Russell passed away peacefully at St. Luke's Hospital on 31st December, 2003. Funeral at Red Cape Cometery, Greenville, today at 4:00 p.m. Cortege will pass St. Anne's Church at 3:00 p.m.

* 湯姆羅素，二〇〇三年十二月三十一日於聖陸克醫院撒手人寰。將於今日下午四時，在格連威爾的紅角墳場下葬。喪禮行列將於今日下午三時經過聖安尼教堂。

第二章　邀請類

　　正式的請帖及覆函都要用第三人稱語氣，而且覆函一定要用手寫。無論應邀或婉辭邀請，都需要儘早做明確的回覆。

Ⅰ.婚禮請帖

1. 正式格式

婚禮的正式請帖

　　婚禮的正式請帖，常用雕版精印的方式。假如要讓朋友們知道婚後的新居住址，可在結婚請帖中附上「新居地址卡」（如圖 p.32）。

> Mr. and Mrs. John Wang
>
> request the honour of your presence
>
> at the marriage of their daughter
>
> Barbara
>
> to
>
> Mr. David Wu
>
> Tuesday, the twenty-first of October
>
> at three o'clock
>
> Holy Family Catholic Church
>
> Taipei
>
> and afterwards at the reception
>
> Grand Hotel
>
> R.S.V.P.

* 王約翰夫婦謹請您於十月二十一日，星期二下午三點，光臨台北天主教聖家堂，參加他們的女兒芭芭拉與吳大衛先生的婚禮，及之後在台北圓山大飯店的招待。謹候回覆。
* R.S.V.P. 「請惠覆」「謹候回覆」
* 上面的格式是請觀禮後連同參加婚禮的，如果只請觀禮而已，則自 and afterwards 這一行起都不寫。

```
******************** 新居地址 ********************
*                                                  *
*                    At Home                       *
*           after the first of January             *
*                2208 Poplar Lane                   *
*                Janesville, Ohio                   *
*                                                  *
******************************************************
```

```
******************** 接受邀請 ********************
*                                                  *
*              Mr. and Mrs. Ted Chen               *
*              accept with pleasure                *
*            Mr. and Mrs. John Wang's              *
*               kind invitation to                 *
*         the marriage of their daughter           *
*                    Barbara                        *
*                      to                           *
*                 Mr. David Wu                      *
*        Tuesday, the twenty-first of October      *
*               at three o'clock                    *
*          Holy Family Catholic Church             *
*                    Taipei                         *
*              and to the reception                 *
*                at Grand Hotel                     *
*                                                  *
******************************************************
```

*　陳泰德夫婦，欣喜接受王約翰先生夫人邀請，將參加他們女兒芭芭拉與吳大衛先生的婚禮，時為十月二十一日星期二下午三點，在台北天主教聖家堂。並參加在圓山大飯店的款待。

*********************** 婉 辭 ***********************

Mr. and Mrs. Ted Chen
regret that they are unable to accept
Mr. and Mrs. John Wang's
kind invitation for
Tuesday, the twenty-first of October

2. 非正式格式

********************* 婚禮邀請函 *********************

February 10, 2003

Dear Emily,

Barbara is being married at home to Jerry Martin, Saturday, March the third, at four-thirty. We hope you will be with us and will be able to stay for the reception afterward.

As ever,

....

*　　芭芭拉將與傑瑞馬丁在家中舉行婚禮，時間是三月三日星期六下午四點半。我們希望你能來，並參加婚禮後的招待會。

接受邀請

January 31, 2003

Dear Alice,

Jack and I wouldn't miss Ann's wedding for anything in the world. You may be sure that we'll be there on Wednesday, February the fifteenth, at four-thirty.

Thank you very much for including us among the friends you want to have with you at this wonderful event.

Affectionately yours,

....

＊ 傑克和我必定會去參加安的婚禮。我們在二月十五日星期三下午四點半，一定會到府上。

非常謝謝你邀請我們參加這次的盛會。

************************ **婉 辭** ************************

March 2, 2003

Dear Mrs. Wu,

Jack and I regret so much that we will not be able to attend Susan's wedding on Monday, June 15th. It is so thoughtful of you to ask us, but unfortunately we have a rather important previous engagement on that day.

We send our very best wishes to Susan and her bridegroom, and we shall be with them in spirit on the happy occasion.

Sincerely,

....

II. 其他邀請函

1. 正式格式

(1) 請 帖

正式請帖可用排印或手寫的方式。

************************ **晚 宴** ************************

Mr. and Mrs. Tom Pan
request the pleasure of your company
at dinner
on Saturday, April the third
at eight o'clock
101 Tung Hwa Street, Taipei

R. S. V. P.

```
******************** 生日酒會 ********************
                    Mr. Walter Wang
          requests the pleasure of the company of
                  Mr. and Mrs. James Lee
                            at
                     a Cocktail Party
                  on the occasion of his
                   Twenty- first Birthday,
               on Tuesday, 21st November, 2003
                   from 6.00 to 8.00 p.m.

          R.S.V.P.                    230 Tung Hua St.
          Tel. 7088283                Taipei
******************************************************
```

      * a cocktail party　雞尾酒會

```
******************** 訂婚酒會 ********************
            Mr. Joe Williamson and Miss  Lily Pan
          request the pleasure of  the  company of
                    Miss Janet Chang
                            at
                     a Cocktail Party
               to celebrate their Engagement
               on Monday, 3rd December, 2003,
                   from 6:00 to 8:00 p.m.

          R.S.V.P.                  102 Hunter Avenue
                                    Brookhaven, Oregon
******************************************************
```

(2) 應邀

接受晚宴邀請

Mr. and Mrs. William Wu
accept with pleasure
the kind invitation of
Mr. and Mrs. Hary Grant
to dinner
on Saturday, April the third
at eight o'clock
101 Tung Hwa Street
Taipei

接受晚宴邀請(二)

Mr. and Mrs. Walter Bryce have much pleasure in
accepting the kind invitation of Mr. and Mrs.
Henry Lin to Dinner on Saturday, 18th May, 2003,
at 8:00 p.m.

接受晚宴邀請(三)

Mr. and Mrs. Walter Bryce thank Mr. and Mrs.
Henry Lin for their kind invitation to Dinner on
Saturday, 18th May, 2003, at 8:00 p.m. and
have much pleasure in accepting.

接受訂婚酒會邀請

Miss Susan Wang congratulates Mr. Joe William and Miss Lily Pan on the occasion of their engagement and has much pleasure in accepting their kind invitation to a cocktail party on Monday, 3rd December, 2003, at 6:00 p.m.

接受雞尾酒會邀請

Mr. and Mrs. Joseph Chang thank Mrs. William Horton very much for her kind invitation to a Cocktail Party on Monday, 1st April, 2003, at 5:30 p.m. and have much pleasure in accepting.

婉辭晚宴

Mr. and Mrs. Joseph Williamson thank Mr. and Mrs. William Au Yeung for their kind invitation to Dinner on Saturday, 18th May, 2003, but very much regret that they are unable to accept because of a previous engagement.

* previous engagement 先前的約會；先約

婉辭訂婚酒會邀請

Miss Janet Pan congratulates Mr. Andrew Tse and Miss Susan Ho on their engagement, but very much regrets that, owing to a previous engagement, she will not be able to accept their kind invitation to a Cocktail Party on Monday, 3rd December, 2003.

2 非正式格式

邀 晚 宴

（Date）

Dear Ted,

　　Joseph and I are planning to have a small dinner party on Friday, 16th February and hope very much that you will be able to come.

　　We are having just a few friends and will be very informal, so please don't dress up. We shall expect you about 8:00p.m.

　　Best wishes,

Yours sincerely,

....

* **dress up** 盛裝

******************* **邀 晚 宴㈡** *******************

（Date）

Dear Mr. Lin,

　　Will you have dinner with us at our home on Wednesday, June the fifteenth, at seven o'clock?

　　It has been a long time since we have had the pleasure of seeing you, and we do hope you will find it possible to be with us.

　　　　　　　　　　Yours sincerely,

　　　　　　　　　　...........

* It has been … to be with us.　好久不見了，我們非常希望你能來。

****************** **邀 晚 宴㈢** ******************

（Date）

Dear Jen,

　　Please say that you and Henry are free on November seventeenth and can dine with us at seven-thirty.　Our dear friends Marie and Eric Gould are to be with us that weekend so we are planning a small dinner party for them— just a few special friends.

　　Walter is looking forward to seeing you both, as I am.

　　　　　　　　　　Affectionately yours,

　　　　　　　　　　..................

邀晚宴（四）

（Date）

Dear Mrs. White,

　　My husband and I should be so pleased if you and your daughter would dine with us next Tuesday at 7:30. I am asking a few other people, and I hope we may have some music after dinner. Mr. Somerset, who is now staying with us, sings extremely well, and if Nellie would only consent to bring her violin with her, I feel sure we should have a most delightful evening.

　　Believe me, dear Mrs. White,

　　　　　　　　Yours sincerely,

　　　　　　　　‥‥‥‥‥‥

* violin〔͵vaɪə′lɪn〕 *n.* 小提琴

****************** 邀 晚 宴 (五) ******************

(Date)

Dear Mary,

　　Knowing of your interest in modern music, I thought of you as soon as I learned I was to have the pleasure of entertaining the Conservatory Quintet. Do join us for dinner and an evening of music on the thirteenth.

　　I hope you can accept, and that seven is a convenient time for you.

　　　　　　　　　　　　Affectionately yours,

　　　　　　　　　　　　.................

* conservatory〔kən'sɜvə͵torɪ〕*n.* 音樂學校
* quintet〔kwɪn'tet〕*n.* 五重奏者；五重唱者

****************** 接受晚宴邀請 ******************

(Date)

Dear Jane,

　　Very many thanks for your invitation to dinner on 16th February. *I am glad to come and look forward to seeing you and* Philip *again.*

　　Best wishes,

　　　　　　　　　　　　Yours sincerely,

　　　　　　　　　　　　...............

****************** **接受晚宴邀請㈡** ****************
（Date）

Dear Ann,

Bert and I are happy to accept your invitation for dinner on Saturday, July 29th, at eight o'clock. We appreciate your asking us, especially since we are to share in such a very special occasion as your silver anniversary.

Cordially yours,

....

* silver anniversary 二十五週年紀念

****************** **接受晚宴邀請㈢** ****************
（Date）

Dear Joan,

Your invitation to my family to join yours for Thanksgiving dinner was greeted with hurrahs from everyone. We're looking forward to seeing you and Tom again.

Following your suggestion, we'll arrive at 4 p.m., with appetites sharpened to a nice edge. ***Thanks so much for this wonderful invitation.***

Affectionately yours,

....

* hurrah〔həˈrɔ〕*interj.* 歡呼聲

************** **婉辭晚宴邀請** **************

(Date)

Dear Peggy,

Thank you very much for inviting me to dinner on 16th February. *I would love to have been able to come*, but I have to leave for Tokyo on that day. *It was very kind of you to ask me*, but I am afraid that under the circumstances I will not be able to come. I hope to see you and Philip when I get back.

Best wishes,

Yours sincerely,

....

* in the circumstances 在此情形之下

************** **婉辭晚宴邀請(二)** **************

(Date)

Dear Mrs. Chang,

Thank you so much for your kind invitation to dinner on Saturday, May 20th. I very much regret that as my husband and I have a previous engagement, we are unable to accept your invitation.

Yours sincerely,

....

****************** 婉辭晚宴邀請㈢ ******************

（Date）

Dear Philip,

　　I have put off writing this note until the last possible moment, hoping that Jack could finish his business on the coast and be back in time for your dinner party. It doesn't seem now that he will be back in time. Of course, you must be told in time to enable you to make other arrangements, and I, therefore, regretfully ask you to please excuse us.

　　It was very sweet of you to ask us. Jack has always enjoyed your parties and I know he will be as sorry to miss this one as I am.

Sincerely,

…………

---

* **_put off_** 延期

* regretfully〔rɪ'grɛtfəlɪ〕*adv.* 感到抱歉地

*
　　爲了希望傑克能完成沿岸的工作，及時趕回來參加你的晚宴，我儘可能延後（晚）寫這封信。但是傑克似乎無法及時趕回來了。當然，我應該及早通知你，好讓你能另做安排。因此，請原諒我們無法參加。

　　謝謝你邀請我們。傑克一直都很喜歡你的宴會，這回我們不能參加，我知道他和我一樣的覺得非常可惜。

邀共進午餐

(Date)

Dear Mrs. Anderson,

How nice that you have planned to stay on here after the holidays！I am having a small luncheon here on Wednesday, the fourteenth, at one o'clock, and I do hope you can come.

Sincerely yours,

....

邀共進午餐(二)

(Date)

Dear Elizabeth,

Mary Holmes of Rockford is coming to stay with me a few days next week. She and I are both hoping you can come to a luncheon here Wednesday, the fourteenth, at one o'clock.

Fondly,

....

************************ 邀共進午餐㈢ *********************

（Date）

Dear Amelia,

　　Will you and John *lunch with us this coming* Saturday, at one o'clock ?

　　Looking forward to seeing you,

Affectionately,

....

****

********************** 邀共進午餐㈣ *********************

（Date）

Dear Ann,

　　Will you have lunch with us at our house on Sunday, March 29, at 12 o'clock ?

　　Jane is coming home by then on spring vacation, and she will be delighted to see you.

　　I do hope you will find it possible to be with us.

Yours fondly,

....

****

*　　三月二十九日星期六，中午十二點，能否請你與我們在家共進午餐？
　　屆時珍將返家度春假，她會很高興與你見面。
　　希望你能與我們相聚。

**************** 接受邀請 ****************

(Date)

Dear Mrs. Wang,

I am delighted to come to your lunch on Sunday, March 29, at 12 o'clock.

Thank you so much for asking me.

I particularly look forward to seeing Jane.

Yours sincerely,

....

**************** 婉　辭 ****************

(Date)

Dear Joan,

We are so sorry that we cannot accept your kind invitation for Saturday *because of another engagement.*

Thank you for thinking of us, and I hope to see you soon.

Sincerely,

....

* 我們非常抱歉，因星期六另有約會，無法接受你好意的邀請。
謝謝你想到我們，我希望很快能再見到你。

* engagement〔ɪnˈgedʒmənt〕n. 約會

邀請雞尾酒會

（Date）

Dear Tony,

　　As you probably already know, George Brown is leaving Taipei to return to the United States. I want to give a little cocktail party for him so that his friends here will have a chance to say good-bye and I hope very much that you will be able to come.

　　We shall start the party at about 6 o'clock and later will probably go out to supper at one of the restaurants on Chung-Shan North Rd. I hope that you will be able to join us for supper as well.

　　Best wishes,

Yours sincerely,

....

* cocktail party 雞尾酒會
* restaurant 〔′rɛstərənt, -, rɑnt 〕 *n.* 飯店；餐館
* As you probably already know … you will be able to come.
  也許你已經知道喬治布朗即將離開台北，回到美國。我將爲他舉行一個小型的雞尾酒會，以便他的朋友們能有機會向他道別。我非常希望你能來。

****************** **應邀雞尾酒會** ******************

(Date)

Dear Jonathan,

Thank you very much for your invitation to your cocktail party for George Brown on May 13th. *I shall love to come*, for I have known George for two years and certainly want to see him again before he leaves us. I think it is a splendid idea to take him out to supper afterwards and I shall also like to join you. Please let me pay a share of the bill.

I look forward to seeing you on the thirteenth.

Yours sincerely,

....

* splendid 〔'splɛndɪd〕 *adj.* 極佳的
* bill 〔bɪl〕 *n.* 帳單

*********************** 邀 茶 敍 ********************

（Date）

Dear Miss Liu,

　　It would give me great pleasure if you would come to tea with me next Thursday at 4:30. It seems quite a long time since I saw you last.

　　　　　　　　　　　　　　　Yours sincerely,

　　　　　　　　　　　　　　　..................

********************* 接受邀請 ********************

（Date）

Dear Mrs. Gates,

　　I accept with great pleasure your kind invitation to tea for Thursday. Yes, it seems a long time since we met. I look forward to hearing all your news.

　　　　　　　　　　　　　　　Yours sincerely,

　　　　　　　　　　　　　　　..................

邀野餐

（Date）

Dear Alfred,

　　Bessie and I are planning a picnic for next Saturday, and we wonder if you will join our party. The idea is that we should all meet here for lunch, and afterwards catch a train for Mt. Ali and have tea in the inn there, or rather in the garden behind the inn. There is a train home about 7, and Mother wants everyone to come back for supper. I think it will be great fun. I am asking about a dozen people in all— the Batesons, Fred Porter, Mary Andrews and her sister, Arthur Saxon, Lena Jones and so on. I think you know them all. Hoping you can come,

　　　　　　　　　　　　　Believe me,
　　　　　　　　　　　　　　Very sincerely yours,
　　　　　　　　　　　　　　．．．．．．．．．．．．．．．．．．．．．．

* inn〔ɪn〕*n.* 旅館；酒店
* *or rather*　更正確的說
* There is a train home about 7.　大約七點左右，有一班回程的火車。
* I am asking about a dozen people in all.　我總共邀請了十來個人。

******************** 接受邀請 ********************

（Date）

Dear Caroline,

I think it's a splendid idea. Thanks awfully for asking me. I accept with great pleasure. I suppose if I turn up at Chiayi about 1 o'clock on Saturday that will be correct. Till then,

Yours ever sincerely,

....

* 我認為那是個妙主意。謝謝你邀請我，我很高興接受。我想我星期六一點到達嘉義應該沒錯吧！
* awfully〔'ɔfʊlɪ〕*adv.* 非常地
* **turn up** 出現；來臨

******************** 接受邀請㈡ ********************

（Date）

Dear Susan,

Thank you so much for asking us. We are delighted to accept your kind invitation.

As you suggested, we will take the ten-thirty train from Taipei this Friday.

Looking forward to seeing you again,

Sincerely,

....

婉 辭

(Date)

Dear Caroline,

I am indeed sorry to say that I cannot accept your kind invitation to the picnic. Wilfrid Gordon was here yesterday and made me promise to spend the weekend with him at his people's house at Guildford. I would much rather have come to your picnic, but I am afraid there's no way out of it now. What a jolly time you will all have!

Yours very sincerely,

....

* people〔'pipl〕*n.* 家族；親戚
* I would much rather … there's no way out of it now. 我寧願去參加你們的野餐，但是恐怕現在已經沒辦法這樣做了。
* jolly〔'dʒɑlɪ〕*adj.* 愉快的

邀來訪並小住

(Date)

Dear Rosa,

Will you come and spend a few days with us here ? My mother asks me to say how glad she would be to see you. If you could come on Friday next to stay till the following Monday week, it would be very jolly. Trains leave Waterloo at frequent intervals during the afternoon, and if you would let me know which one you propose to catch, I would come and meet you at the station. You remember what fun we had when you were with us last year ? The Tooley girls are still here, and I think we shall be able to get up some hockey and possibly some dancing in the evenings. I do hope you will be able to come.

Yours affectionately,
....

* interval〔'ɪntəvḷ〕n.（時間的）間隔
* get up 準備
* hockey〔'hɑkɪ〕n. 曲棍球

********************** 邀朋友來玩 **********************

（Date）

Dear Jack,

　　How about spending the New Year's holiday
with us ? Since it's a long holiday you could arrive
on Friday for dinner and leave Monday after lunch.

　　The country will do you good and you can
get in some golf.

With love

....

*　　　元旦的假期和我們一起過如何？你可以星期五來午餐，然後星期一
午飯後走。鄉村生活對你有好處，而且你可以玩高爾夫球。

********************** 婉 辭 **********************

（Date）

Dear Elizabeth,

　　*You cannot imagine my disappointment at not
being able to accept your* charming *invitation.* On
Tuesday I am going to Tainan to stay with my aunt,
Mrs. Wu, for a fortnight, so of course it is quite
impossible for me to come to you. I am so disappointed. Best love to your mother,

Sincerely,

....

* fortnight〔'fɔrtnaɪt〕*n.* 兩星期

Ⅲ.取消邀請

正式的格式

```
Mr. and Mrs. Henry Chen regret that,
owing to the death of Mrs. Chen's mother, they
are obliged to recall their invitation for Wednes-
day, the third of June.
```

非正式格式

（Date）

Dear Joan,

As you may have heard, John's grandmother
has been taken to the hospital. Naturally, all of
us are very worried about her.

Under the circumstances, I have called off
the dinner party we had planned for Wednesday,
the third of March. I know you will understand.

I will be in touch with you again soon.

As ever,

....

---

*　　也許你已經聽說約翰的祖母入院了。大家自然都很爲她擔心。

在此情形下，我必須取消原定三月三日星期三的晚宴。我知道你會
了解的。

我會很快的再與你聯絡。

* call off　取消

Ⅳ.延期邀請

正式的格式

********************* 晚宴延期 *********************

Mr. and Mrs. Bill Pan regret that it is necessary to postpone their invitation to dinner on Monday, November the sixth to Friday, November the twenty-fourth, at seven o'clock Mandarin Hotel.

* 　潘比爾夫婦抱歉，必須將他們在十一月六日星期三的晚宴邀請，延期至十一月二十四日七點，在中泰賓館舉行。
* postpone〔post′pon〕*vt.* 延擱
* Mandarin Hotel 中泰賓館

11月16日 ➡ 11月24日

非正式的格式

（Date）

Dear Janet,

Since Paul has been called to settle some business in Hong Kong by the head office, the dinner party we had planned for Tuesday, the tenth of May, has been postponed to Thursday, the nineteenth of May, at seven o'clock. I hope you will understand and do try to make it.

Looking forward to seeing you soon.

Sincerely,

....

* 　由於保羅被總公司派到香港去處理事務，我們原定五月十日星期二舉行的晚宴，改期至五月十九日星期四七點舉行。希望你能了解並能前來。

　　盼望很快能見到你。

第三章 致賀類

祝賀信應表現誠懇眞摯的祝福，現今市面上雖有各類的賀卡，但是親筆致賀，更令人倍感溫馨。致賀信在獲知消息後，越早寄出越好，不宜拖延。

(1)賀生日

賀 生 日

February 14, 2003

Dear Ted,

　　Congratulations on this happy day. The best of all good things for this birthday and all the many more to come.

Sincerely yours,

....

賀 生 日 ㈡

February 10，2003

Dear Isabel,

If only you lived a little closer I could come and bring my happy birthday wishes to you in person. But I will do the next best thing and send you my love, congratulations, and warmest wishes for this day and every day.

Fondly,

....

賀 生 日 ㈢

February 6，2003

Dear Fred,

May I join your many friends and admirers in wishing you a happy birthday? I have held dear your friendship during the last ten years and I look forward to enjoying it for many years to come. Here's hoping you have many, many happy birthdays in store for you. With affectionate birthday wishes,

Sincerely,

....

* May I … a happy birthday？　我可以與你的朋友及你的崇拜者共同恭祝你生日快樂嗎？
* Here's … in store for you.　在此願你擁有無窮盡的快樂生日。

(2) 賀訂婚

賀 訂 婚

(Date)

Dear Ann,

　　We all rejoice with you on the occasion of your son Edward's *engagement, and wish you and* Ted *ever increasing happiness.*

Sincerely,

…………

* on the occasion of　在…之際

賀 訂 婚 (二)

(Date)

Dear Ted,

　　I must just write this line to congratulate you most heartily on your engagement to Miss Crawford.　I only heard of it last night, or I should have written earlier.　I do think you are a lucky fellow.　When do you propose to get married?　When are you coming over for a game of golf?　Now I understand why we've seen so little of you lately!

Yours ever,

…………

* heartily 〔 ′hɑrtɪlɪ 〕 *adv.* 誠懇地

* I only heard … earlier.　我昨晚才聽到這個消息，否則我應該早一點寫信祝賀你。

賀 訂 婚 ㈢

（Date）

Dear Lisa,

The best of luck to you and Barton !

I heard the good news of your engagement this morning and you just can't imagine how pleased I am. Everything I've heard about Barton points to his having the qualities that make an excellent husband. *I can't think of two people more suited to each other than you and Barton.*

Mother joins me in sending best wishes and in offering an invitation to bringing Barton to see us soon. Please send him our congratulations and sincere good wishes.

Affectionately,

....

* Everything … Barton . 我所聽到有關巴頓的每一件事情，在在都顯示出他會是個好丈夫。
我無法找出比你和巴頓更適合的一對了。

賀訂婚㈣

（Date）

Dearest Jane,

    I was delighted to read in the Central Daily News of your engagement to John and I want to wish you both all the happiness in the world.

    Having known you and John for quite a long time now, I am more than happy that you have taken this important step as *I feel certain you are just right for each other.*

           With love,

           …………

* I am … for each other. 我相信你們是最適合的一對，因此非常高興你完成了這件大事。

賀訂婚 ㈤

(Date)

Dear Rosa,

I was delighted to read in the Central Daily News of your engagement to Jim Wang and I would like to send you my warmest congratulations.

I have met your fiancé only once and I would very much like to do so again. My wife and I will be very pleased if you both would like to go out with us to a restaurant so that we can celebrate. Perhaps you would like to suggest a day that would suit you.

As one who has been married for over ten years, I would like to wish you both many years of happiness together.

Yours sincerely,

....

* I have met ... again.　我與你的未婚夫只見過一次面，非常希望能再見到他。

賀 訂 婚 ㈥

（Date）

Dear Emily,

The announcement of your engagement to Samuel Smith is happy news. Although I do not have the privilege of knowing him, *I am sure that if he is your choice he must be a wonderful person.*

My very best wishes on this happy event,

Sincerely,

…………

* privilege〔ˊprɪvlɪdʒ〕*n.* 特殊的榮幸
* Although … knowing him … 雖然我沒有這份榮幸能認識他…

(3) 賀結婚

賀 結 婚

（Date）

Dear Jack,

My blessing, congratulations and good wishes. I wish you the best of everything for all the years ahead.

Fondly,

………

賀 結 婚 ㈡

（Date）

Dear Michael,

Amy and I were delighted to receive the announcement of your marriage in today's mail.

Please accept our most sincere congratulations and very best wishes for all the good fortunes in the world.

Cordially,

....

賀 結 婚 ㈢

（Date）

Dear Henry,

I am delighted to hear of your recent marriage and now send you and your wife my warmest congratulations and best wishes for a very happy married life together.

I hope that when you have settled down in your new home you will bring your wife to see me, for I look forward very much to meeting her.

I am sending you a small present with this letter and I hope you and your wife will find it of some use.

With my best wishes to you both,

Yours sincerely,

....

賀結婚㈣

(Date)

Dear Amy,

It seems only yesterday that you told me you were engaged, and now you are going to be married. I haven't met your handsome fiancé yet, but from everything I have heard, *I know that both of you suit each other perfectly and will surely have a very happy marriage life*.

Please convey my congratulations to your John, and accept my best wishes to the two of you for a marriage filled with all the good things in life.

Sincerely,

....

* fiancé〔ˌfiən'se〕 *n.* 未婚夫

⑷ 賀嬰兒誕生

賀嬰兒誕生

（Date）

Dear Grace,

　　We rejoice with you and wish your daughter a long and happy and meaningful life.

Sincerely yours,

....

---

* rejoice〔rɪˈdʒɔɪs〕*vi.* 高興；歡喜

賀嬰兒誕生㈡

（Date）

Dear Ruth,

　　Mr. Chen joins with me in congratulating you and Mr. Lee on the birth of your son. We are delighted by the news that mother and son are doing well. *May the new heir have a long, healthy and meaningful life!*

Sincerely yours,

....

---

* We are delighted … well. 我們很高興獲知母子均安的消息。

賀嬰兒誕生(三)

（Date）

Dear Mr. Lee,

It seems like only yesterday that I congratulated you on your marriage. And now, in the twinkling of an eye, I am congratulating you on the birth of a son.

I am sure that the little stranger must look very much like the old Mr. Lee. Many years later, he will be as bright a boy as my classmate, his father, in the primary school.

I hope I shall very soon have the pleasure of visiting the old and the little Mr. Lee.

Sincerely yours,

....

* in the twinkling of an eye 轉眼之間

⑸ **賀畢業**

賀　畢　業

（Date）

Dear Jack,

　　Your graduation has great meaning to me particularly because of my close friendship with your parents.

　　I extend my best wishes and congratulations to you.

　　I hope that you will find it possible to continue your studies and develop the talents and skills with which you are abundantly endowed. May I add that there is no implication of finality to the word "graduation." On the contrary, according to Webster's Collegiate Dictionary, the basic definition of the word "graduate" is "to pass by degrees ; to change gradually."

　　May you have health, happiness and outstanding success in all your ventures.

　　　　　　　　　Sincerely,

　　　　　　　　　…………

---

* extend〔ɪkˈstɛnd〕vt. 給予
* endow〔ɪnˈdaʊ〕vt. 賦與；天賦
* implication〔͵ɪmplɪˈkeʃən〕n. 含意
* finality〔faɪˈnælətɪ〕n. 完結
* I hope … to change gradually. 我希望你將會繼續你的學業，發揮天生的許多才藝。容我補充一點，亦即「畢業」並不意味著結束；相反的，根據韋氏大學字典，「畢業」的根本意義是「逐漸地改變」。
* outstanding〔aʊtˈstændɪŋ〕adj. 顯著的

賀 畢 業 (二)

（Date）

Dear George,

　　This is a notable day in your life and, of course, for your parents, relatives and friends. Graduation is a time for rejoicing and I rejoice with you on this happy occasion.

　　It is also a time for reflection. You will be going out into the world to make a career for yourself. You stand on the threshold of what I hope will be a happy life and a rewarding career.

　　I wish you well in all your undertakings and hope that you will find your career a source of great joy and happiness.

　　　　　　　　　　　　Sincerely,

　　　　　　　　　　　　…………

* reflection〔rɪˈflɛkʃən〕 *n.* 內省；考慮
* threshold〔ˈθrɛʃold〕 *n.* 開始
* rewarding〔rɪˈwɔrdɪŋ〕 *adj.* 有用的；有益的
* It is also … a rewarding career. 這也是要深思熟慮的時刻。你即將開創你的前途，我希望這將是你快樂如意的人生的開端。

賀 畢 業 ㈢

（Date）

Dear Joe,

Congratulations! Earning your Master's degree is an achievement of note, and I hope you are feeling proud and happy — as you deserve.

I'm hopeful and confident, too, that the graduation ceremonies will really be a "Commencement" and that satisfying and rewarding experiences await you.

Sincerely,

....

---

* of note 重要的；引人矚目的

* commencement 〔kə'mɛnsmənt〕 *n.* 開始；畢業典禮

* Earning your Master's degree … as you deserve. 獲得碩士學位是一項引人矚目的成就。我希望你爲此感到驕傲和歡欣，因爲這是你應得的。

* I'm hopeful … await you. 我希望同時也相信畢業是一個開端，稱心如意的事物正在前面等著你。

⑹ 賀金榜提名

賀考試及格

（Date）

My dear Joe,

It is with the most sincere pleasure I write to congratulate you on the passing of your examination. I saw the lists in today's paper, and was so very glad to notice how well you had passed. *It is a great thing to know that all your hard work has had such a successful result.* I hope you will soon come round and tell us all about it.

Yours sincerely,

....

* come round 來訪

賀通過考試

（Date）

Dear Roger,

I have just seen from the Examination Pass List that you have passed with excellent results. I am delighted about this and *I am sure that it is a well deserved reward for all the hard work you have done* during the past year.

Now that you have got this excellent result I am sure that you will be able to do well in your work and I send you my best wishes for the future.

With very many congratulations,

Yours sincerely,

....

賀通過律師考試

（Date）

Dear Henry,

　　I noted in this morning's newspapers that your name is on the list of those who passed the Bar examinations.

　　My congratulations and my best wishes that you have health, happiness and outstanding success in the practice of law, and many years to enjoy it.

Sincerely,

…………

* bar〔bɑr〕*n.* 律師
* practice〔'præktɪs〕*n.* 業務

(7) 賀升遷

賀 升 遷

（Date）

Dear Allen,

I've just heard the good news. *Congratulations. Ability such as yours can't be hidden for long. I'm sure this promotion is just a stepping-stone to even greater things.* I can imagine how proud Penny must be of you. Good luck in the new job.

Sincerely,

....

* promotion 〔prə'moʃən〕 *n*. 升遷
* stepping‑stone 〔'stɛpɪŋˌston〕 *n*. 踏腳石；進身之階
* Ability … even greater things. 如你這般的才華是不會長久埋沒的。
  我相信這回的昇遷，只是未來更輝煌的成就的階梯而已。

賀升遷㈡

(Date)

Dear Harry,

　　I am delighted to hear of your promotion to Assistant Manager in the Sales Department. Very many congratulations！All of us who have seen you at work know that you owe your promotion to the hard work you have done for the last five years. You must be very proud of yourself and I think that you have every reason to be.

　　I am sure that you will find your new work enjoyable and exciting and I look forward to hearing of your next success.

　　With many congratulations and my best wishes for the future,

　　　　　　　　　　　　Yours sincerely,
　　　　　　　　　　　　·················

* owe your promotion to the hard work you have done 把你的升遷，歸功於勤奮的工作。
* You have every reason to be. 你當之無愧。

賀升遷 (三)

（Date）

Dear Mr. Chang,

It was with a feeling of extreme pleasure that I read of your promotion to assistant manager of the Dow office. It is a promotion that you really deserve.

I wish you the best of luck in your new position. I know I will be reading more good news about you in the trade papers.

Very cordially,

....

(8) 賀獲獎

賀 獲 獎

（Date）

Dear Tom,

I was delighted to hear that you won second prize in the Contest. It must feel good to know that you ranked among the best in a state-wide contest.

All of your friends are proud of you.

Cordially,

....

(9) 賀獲殊榮

賀獲殊榮

（Date）

Dear Mrs. Liu,

　　All of us at the office take great pleasure in sending congratulations to you for winning the Women's Club Citation. I know of no one who deserves it more than you.

　　Our very best wishes to you,

　　　　　　　　　　Sincerely,

　　　　　　　　　　…………

　　* citation〔saɪ'teʃən〕 *n*. 獎狀；褒獎

(10) 賀喬遷

賀　喬　遷

（Date）

Dear Amy,

　　May happiness and good health attend you and your family in your new house.

　　I know this is a busy and exciting time for you, and I'm going to give you an opportunity to get settled before I come to call, but I just couldn't wait to express good wishes from George and me.

　　　　　　　　　　Affectionately yours,

　　　　　　　　　　……………………

第四章　問候類

　　問候信能使彼此的情誼更密切，不可不寫。不必太嚴肅，也不要訴苦。要愉快、親切，像與對方說話一般，述說生活的點滴、趣事或周圍人們的消息。佳節問候，更是增進情誼的最好方式。

Ⅰ．一般問候

給爸媽

（Date）

Dear Ma and Dad,

　　I apologize for being a day late with my weekly letter to you but I have been working overtime at the office this week and have arrived home very tired each evening.

　　Thank you so much for your letter, which arrived as usual on Wednesday morning. I am so glad that your cold is better, Dad. But I hope you will not attempt to return to the office until you are quite free from it.

　　There is nothing of much interest to report this week except that last Friday afternoon, the director asked me a few personal questions and showed approval of my work. One of the colleagues informed me that it is a good sign. Maybe I am under consideration for promotion. Anyway, we shall see.

I think I shall not be able to come home for Thanksgiving, as the work is still pressing, but I do think I can make it up at Christmas. I will tell you the exact time of my return.

Give my love to Connie.

Your loving son,

....

* 很抱歉，每週和您們通一次的信，這次遲了一天才寫。因爲這個禮拜我在公司加班，每晚回到家都很累。

和往常一樣，我星期三早上收到您們的來信，謝謝您們。很高興爸爸您的感冒好些了，不過希望在您沒有完全好前，不要回公司上班。

這個禮拜沒有什麼特別的事，可以告訴您們，除了上星期五下午，上司問了我一些私人的問題，並對我的工作表示稱許。有一位同事告訴我，這是好預兆，可能他們在考慮擢升我。不管怎麼樣，我們總會知道的。

我想感恩節我沒有辦法回家了，因爲工作還很趕。不過聖誕節我可以回去。我會事先告訴您們我回去的確切時間。

代我問候康妮。

* overtime〔'ovɚ,taɪm〕*adv*. 超出時間地
* **be free from** 無～的；免於；無～之憂的
* Thanksgiving〔,θæŋks'gɪvɪŋ〕*n*. 感恩節（十一月最後的星期四）

給 妹 妹

（Date ）

Dear Sis,

　　We have been having a taste here of the kind of weather I always associate with Taipei. That got me to thinking about Mom and Dad and, naturally, of you and Bill. You can imagine how pleased I was to find your letter in the mailbox.

　　It is great to hear all the news about the family and Tainan. Compared with you, I am leading a pretty tame life. I ran into Simon just the other week ; he has not changed a bit since he was the leader of the gang when we were children together.

　　Talking about Simon, I remember that he said Bill was thinking about going into the Government service. I think Bill might do well to drop Simon a line. He is a particularly well-informed fellow, and has quite a few influential friends. His address is 52 Tai Ping Road, Taichung.

　　It has been a long time since I have seen you. I am saving my days off so that I shall have a long vacation in the summer. I hope I shall see both you and Bill then.

　　Send my love to Dad and Mom and tell them I will write to them a few days later.

　　　　　　　　　　As ever,

　　　　　　　　　　………

　　＊　　我們這裡最近的天氣總是讓我聯想起台北，讓我想起媽媽和爸爸，自然也想起妳和比爾。妳可以想像，我在信箱裡看到妳的信時，有多高興。

　　所有家裡和台南的消息，都令人興奮。和妳比起來，我的生活平淡多了。就是上個禮拜，我碰到賽門，他一點也沒有變，還是當年我們這群小蘿蔔頭的頭頭的樣子。

　　說到賽門，記得妳提過，比爾想進公家機關。我想比爾最好和賽門捎個信，他的消息非常靈通，還有不少有勢力的朋友。他的地址是台中市太平路 52 號。

　　好久沒看到妳了。我現在放假的日子也工作，這樣夏天我就可以有個長假。希望到時候可以看到妳和比爾。

　　代我問候爸爸、媽媽，告訴他們，我過幾天會寫信給他們。

* taste〔test〕*n.* 風味；情趣
* *drop one a line* 給某人捎個信
* *do well to*＋*V* 以～爲宜；～比較好
* well-informed〔'wɛlɪn'fɔrmd〕*adj.* 消息靈通的
* influential〔,ɪnflʊ'ɛnʃəl〕*adj.* 有勢力的；有影響的
* day-off〔'de'ɔf〕*n.* 休息日

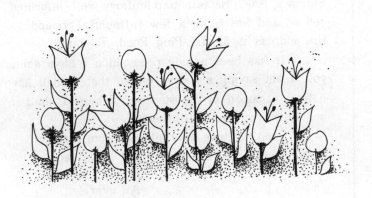

給叔叔嬸嬸

(Date)

Dear Aunt May and Uncle Tom,

I felt sorry to have missed your visit to our home last Sunday. I had wanted to go home for Thanksgiving, but circumstances prevented me from doing that. Has Mother told you all about me？ If not, then I'll tell you now.

First of all, I must thank you both for the wonderful present. The suede gloves fit me like my own skin, and they are very soft and warm. I really appreciate the thoughtfulness.

I am doing quite all right. I have grown accustomed to office work and its schedule. But I have not quite gotten used to living all by myself, taking meals in a small café and living in a dingy hostel, etc. I miss Mom's cooking and yours, too, Aunt May.

How's your business, Uncle Tom？ Do you still go fishing in the afternoons？ Remember the time you helped me catch my first fish？ I still want to thank you for teaching me swimming and rowing.

I wonder if you are still writing poems, Auntie. And if you are, won't you give me the pleasure of reading them?

I hope all is well with you. My love to you both,

With love,

....

---

* 我很遺憾，上星期天您們來我們家玩時，我不在。我原想感恩節回家的，可是情況並不允許我那樣做。想必媽媽已經把我的一切，告訴您們了？如果沒有，我現在就告訴您們！

首先，我要謝謝您們兩位，送我那麼好的禮物。麂皮手套很合手，又很柔軟、暖和。眞謝謝您們的關心。

我的一切都很好，對公司的工作和作息，也漸漸習慣了。只是我還不太習慣孤零零的一個人在小餐館裡吃飯、住在昏暗的招待所…等。我想念媽媽和嬸嬸您做的菜。

湯姆叔叔，您的生意好嗎？您每天下午，還去釣魚嗎？記得那次，您幫我釣到我的第一條魚，我還要謝謝您教我游泳和划船。

嬸嬸，不知道您還寫不寫詩，如果寫的話，能否讓我欣賞呢？

希望您們一切都順利，謹致我對您們兩位的敬愛。

* suede〔swed〕 *adj*. 麂皮製成的
* thoughtfulness〔'θɔtfəlnɪs〕 *n*. 細心；體貼；關切
* cafe〔kə'fe,kæ'fe〕 *n*. 飲食店；飯館
* dingy〔'dɪndʒɪ〕 *adj*. 昏暗的；骯髒的
* hostel〔'hɑstl̩〕 *n*. 招待所（特指爲青年所設而不以盈利爲目的者）

給老師

（Date ）

Dear Sir,

It has been almost two years since I left school. I must apologize for not having written to you. I hope you are getting on very well and all that you have undertaken is successful.

As my father could not afford my entering a university, I work with a book shop where aside from scheduled work, I can do reading alone at night. And I am saving money, hoping to get a college education some day.

If you are not very busy, I shall like to hear from you.

Trusting you are in the best of health,

I remain

Respectfully yours,

....

*　　　很抱歉，畢業都快兩年了，卻一直沒有寫信問候您。希望您身體健康，事事順利。

由於我父親無法供我唸大學，我在一家書店工作，除了日常的工作外，晚上我可以自己讀書，我在存錢，希望將來能完成大學教育。

如果您不太忙的話，我很想知道您的近況。

敬祝安康。

給搬走的隣居

(Date)

Dear Nora,

The big news here is our car. Kate, Lisa, and I finally convinced Joe that the old tin can would fall to pieces if it was driven up Yangmingshan once more. But just wait till you read what my serious, conservative husband bought — a bright bright-and-yellow hard-top convertible with white-wall tires and leather upholstery! The kids are in seventh heaven and, frankly, I'm pretty thrilled myself.

Joe gets his vacation in June, so don't be surprised to see this vision on wheels come honking at your front door.

And as if that wasn't excitement enough, Carl Evans came home from his study overseas with a wife! Dora's a lovely girl who lived next door to him in America. They have rented the little yellow house on the corner of Tung Hwa Garden. We were over for a buffet dinner Friday night, and can Dora cook! We all kissed our diets good-bye that night. I am enclosing her recipe for a wonderful cake called plum cake. I've tried it, and it just melts in your mouth.

Aside from the usual drugstore gossip to the effect that Jane Newsom is going steady with Gene Broder and that Mrs. Mann has painted her house shocking pink, there is nothing new here.

Let us hear all about Gerald. I'm sure Jack loves his new job, since nothing but a chance to work on *China Daily News* could have induced you all to move away. We really do miss you, so please write a long, long letter.

Affectionately,

....

---

* The big news here ⋯ at your front door.

　　大新聞，我們買車了！我、凱特、麗莎終於使喬相信，如果那輛老罐頭車再開上陽明山，將會碎掉。你聽聽，我那嚴肅而保守的丈夫買了什麼——一輛鮮黃、藍色的硬頂摺蓬跑車外帶白色的輪胎和皮製的椅墊。孩子們樂壞了，說真的，我也很興奮。

　　喬六月有假，所以看了我們坐車到你門前按喇叭，不要驚訝。

* tin can　一般謔稱的罐頭車
* hard-top convertible　硬頂的摺蓬跑車
* upholstery〔ʌpˈholstərɪ〕*n*. 椅套；椅墊
* *in seventh heaven*　很興奮；樂壞了
* thrill〔θrɪl〕*vi*. 因興奮而激動
* honk〔hɔŋk, hɑŋk〕*vt*. 按（汽車喇叭）
* *next door to*～　在～隔壁
* buffet〔buˈfe, ˈbʌfɪt〕*n*. 自助餐
* plum cake　加葡萄乾的糕餅
* drugstore　雜貨店（出售藥品、化粧品、香煙、清涼飲料等，爲一種社交場所）
* *to the effect that*～　大意是說～

給朋友

（ Date ）

Dear Emily,

Recalling the wonderful summer our families shared at Keelung, I suddenly realized I hadn't written you since last spring. I hope you and Greg and the children have had a good vacation. Did Clare get a lovely, smooth coat of tan again? And how is Teddy's diving coming?

Jackie has just come back from camp. I think it was a happy and good experience for him.

I'd love to hear from you when you have a moment to write. In the meantime, I send my love.

Affectionately,

....

---

* Did Clare get a lovely, smooth coat of tan again? And how is Teddy's diving coming? 克萊兒的皮膚，是否又晒成美麗平滑的褐色？泰迪的潛水，練得如何？

給 朋 友(二)

（Date ）

Dear Tracy,

On Saturday I used your recipe for that delicious stewed lotus nuts with sugar candy, and served it to the bridge club. It was a great success, and I thought how nice it would have been to have you with us.

Have you joined a bridge club since moving to Taipei? Do let me know how you and the family are, and if you are enjoying the new house.

Affectionately,

....

* recipe〔ˊrɛsəpɪ〕*n.* 食譜
* stewed lotus nuts with sugar candy 冰糖蓮子

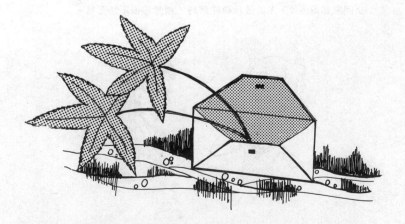

給 朋 友㈡

（ Date ）

Dear Jeff,

    Sorry I haven't written for a long time but I have been very busy. How are you？

    Last month I moved because I had a quarrel with my landlady. I was very upset because she wouldn't give me a key to the house. It was very embarrassing to ring on the door every time I came home, especially when I wanted to be late.

    My new home is great. I would be glad if you would come and see me.

                Affectionately,

                 …………

* Last month I moved … when I wanted to be late. 上個月我搬家了，因為我和女房東吵架。我很煩她不肯給我房子的鑰匙，害得我每次回家都得按鈴，尤其是我要晚歸時，總覺得很不好意思。

給 朋 友(四)

（Date ）

Dear Mrs. Jason,

　　　Did you have a wonderful summer? I hope so. Looking over my snapshots brings back many of the high points of the summer. One of the best was the trip along the East-West Highway. Here are a few of my favorite shots.

　　　　　　　　　　Sincerely yours,

　　　　　　　　　　·················

* 　　你夏天過得好玩嗎？希望是。看了一些照片，讓我回想起夏天的高潮，最好玩的是東西橫貫公路的行程。這裡附上我最喜愛的幾張照片。
* snapshot〔′snæp‚ʃɑt〕*n.* 快相；快照

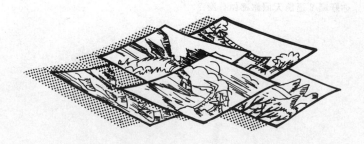

給 朋 友㈤

（ Date ）

Dear Jane,

Thanks for your Christmas card. It was very pretty.

Did you have a nice Christmas？ I'm sorry I haven't written, but the family was very busy at Christmas, and I have been studying for my exams.

How are you? What did you do during the holidays？

Give my love to all the family.

Love,

......

* 謝謝你漂亮的聖誕卡。

你聖誕節過得快樂嗎？很抱歉，沒有在聖誕節前寄卡片給你。因爲家裏很忙，我也爲考試而忙著準備功課。

你好嗎？這幾天假你都做什麽？

給國外的友人

May 12, 2003

Dear Oscar,

How's life in America? I hope things are as good for you as they are for me.

Taipei sure is treating me right lately. Business is booming! The profits of my toy company have doubled in the last fiscal year. The Christmas demand in America sure helped us out; I've never seen anything sell like those "Barbie" dolls.

Instead of reinvesting my capital in toys, I've decided to go into electronics. Yes, Oscar, I've diversified!

My wife says to say hello. Did I tell you she'll have another baby in June?

I hope it's a girl this time.

Well, I've got to get back to work. Take care!

Best wishes,

....

* booming〔'bumɪŋ〕 *adj.* 發展迅速的
* reinvest〔,rɪɪn'vɛst〕 *vt.* 再投資
* diversify〔də'vɜsə,faɪ, daɪ-〕 *vi.* 作多樣性投資
* My wife says to say hello. 內人問候您。

給國外的友人㈡

(Date)

Dear Henry,

Last night Tom and Bill dropped in and we had real riotous time, just like the old times except you were not here. Then we all talked about you and wondered what you were doing at that moment. Could it be possible that you were writing us a letter?

Half a year has gone by since we said farewell to each other at the airport. Although we have gotten a few hurriedly scribbled postcards, you have not written us a decent letter long enough to tell us what is going on with you.

What kind of life are you living in a foreign place? Is it different from our place? Is school keeping you busy? Or have you fallen in love with a pretty blonde already? Your friends here are most anxious to know about you, so will you let me have the privilege to give them the news first-hand?

I am working with the firm, as usual, just one of a billion wage slaves. Paul has married Jenny. No surprise to you, I presume.

Chinese New Year is creeping up now. How do you feel about it?

With best wishes,

Sincerely,

....

* 　　昨晚湯姆和比爾順道來訪，我們如往日一般開懷的胡鬧了一陣，只可惜你不在。我們談起你，都想知道那一刻你在做什麼。會不會正在寫信給我們？

　　機場道別至今，已經半年了。在此期間，你除了寄來幾張匆忙潦草的明信片外，就不曾寫過一封像樣的長信，告訴我們你的近況。

　　你在外國的生活如何？與我們的有何不同？學校課業忙嗎？還是你已經愛上一位金髮美女？這裏的朋友都很想知道你的近況，能否讓我以第一手的消息告訴他們？

　　我和以往一樣在公司上班，是億萬個薪水奴隸中的一個。保羅和珍妮結婚了，你不會感到意外吧！

　　春節悄悄來臨了，有何感想？

　　祝安好。

* **drop in** 順道拜訪；偶然來訪
* riotous〔′raɪətəs〕*adj*. 放縱的；恣情的
* farewell〔′fɛr′wɛl , ,fɛr′wɛl〕*n*. 離別；告別辭
* scribble〔′skrɪbḷ〕*vt*. 潦草書寫；胡亂寫
* decent〔′disṇt〕*adj*. 適當的；尚佳的
* blonde〔blɑnd〕*n*. 金髮碧眼的白人女性
* privilege〔′prɪvḷɪdʒ〕*n*. 特別的榮譽
* creep〔krip〕*vi*.（時間等）不知不覺地來臨或消逝

給國外的友人㈢

（Date ）

Dear Paul,

It seems a long time since I was last in England. I have been at my parents' home for two months now, but I still think about London and all the friends I made.

I stopped in Greece on my way home and had a very good time. It's a very interesting country.

There have been a lot of changes here since I left. Many of my friends have got married and have jobs. I suppose I will have to start looking for a job soon, too.

Please write soon. Why don't you come and visit Taiwan? You are always welcome and we have plenty of room.

Take care.

Sincerely,

………

* There have been a lot of changes … have plenty of room.

自我離開後，這裏有了很大的轉變。我幾個朋友都有了工作，並且結婚了。我想我也應該快找個工作了。

你何不到臺灣來玩，我們無論何時都歡迎你，而且也有足夠的房間。希望你儘速回信。

給國外的友人㈣

（Date ）

Dear Mary,

　　Hi！ How are you? How is your life in the United States? Are you going to get married to your old boyfriend? How is your family?

　　I'm sorry I haven't written you for such a long time. I just finished writing my master's thesis this June, getting my Master's Degree in Foreign Literature only this June 17th. Since then, I've been looking for a job and doing some things for my family. I never have any time to get some rest！ I hope that I won't have to make you wait so long for one of my letters again. I promise to write you the very day I get your next letter.

　　Well, I know that this is a short letter, but I just got a phone call to go in for a job interview. So, let me get this mailed off to you rather than make you wait any longer.

　　　　　　　　　　Affectionately,
　　　　　　　　　　Sharon

　　* 　　嗨！在美國的生活過得好嗎？要和你的老男朋友結婚了吧？你家人好嗎？

　　抱歉，這麼久沒有寫信給你，我六月才寫完碩士論文，六月十七日才得到外文碩士學位。從那時候，我就開始找工作，還幫家裏做些事，一直都沒有休息時間。希望下次不會再讓你等那麼久才收到信。下次保證收到你的信當天就回。

　　好了，我知道這封信很短，不過我剛剛接到一個電話，約好面談。所以我先把信寄了，免得你又等太久。

* thesis〔'θisɪs〕*n.* 論文

給 筆 友

（Date）

Dear Pete,

I am very pleased to have this chance to write to you, for I would like to learn about life in Hong Kong and I can tell you something about life here. I therefore hope that you will also want to write to me, for we can learn so much from each other.

I live here in Taipei. This is a cultural city where you may eat all kinds of Chinese food, and go to museums, etc. I am seventeen years old and have a younger sister, Lucy, who is thirteen. My father is a businessman in Taoyuan, which is about forty kilometers away. Every morning he has to leave home early to go there by train and then he comes home in the evening. My mother does not go out to work, but she looks after us all very well.

I go to a local secondary school and I am studying Arts subjects, such as English, History and Geography. I hope to go to university when I leave school, but I will have to work very hard. What subjects do you study at your school?

Every summer holiday our family goes away for a holiday. We usually go by car and tour the island. It is always fun to visit other cities. I hope that one day I will be able to visit Hong Kong, but I am afraid that it is very far away and the air fare is very expensive. Do you think you will be able to visit me in Taipei? I hope so.

> Do please write to me to tell me about life in Hong Kong and then I shall write to you again.
>
> With my best wishes,
>
> Yours sincerely,
>
> ....

* I am very pleased … all very well.

　　我很高興有這個機會寫信給你，因為我希望能多了解香港一點，而我也可以告訴你一些這裏的生活狀況，因此我希望你也寫信給我，這樣我們彼此都可以增加更多的見聞。

　　我住台北，台北是文化中心，在這裏你可以吃到各式各樣的中國菜，及參觀博物館等等。我今年 17 歲，有個妹妹 13 歲，名叫露西。我父親在離台北 40 公里的桃園做生意，他每天都一大早就得離家搭車上班，而傍晚才能回到家。我母親沒有外出工作，她把我們照顧得無微不至。

* cultural center　文化中心

* air fare　機票

給 筆 友㈡

（Date ）

Dear Joseph,

Thank very much for your letter. I was very pleased to hear from you, for I am anxious to know more about life in England *and so I hope that you will write to me more often. I shall certainly write to you to tell you about* Taiwan. *It will be fun having a friend on the other side of the world and I look forward to seeing you in* Taiwan *one day.*

My family and I live in Taipei. My father works as an accountant for a big foreign company and my mother is a teacher. I have one sister and she is a secretary working for a company here. I am studying in a big secondary school that is run by some Roman Catholic priests. It is a good school and many of the boys go to university when they leave. I want to go to university too, but it is very difficult to do so in Taiwan for there are not enough places for all those who want to study in university.

I once went to Hong Kong with my parents for a holiday, but it is too expensive to go far away from Taiwan, and so there are not many countries that we can go to. However, we all enjoy life here in Taiwan, and I think that many foreign tourists like to come here too.

I hope that you will write to me again soon and then I will tell you more about life here in my next letter.

With my best wishes,

Yours sincerely,

....

* Thank you very much … who want to study here.

非常謝謝你的來信。我很高興接到你的信，因為我急於想知道英國的生活情況，也希望你能多來信。當然我也會告訴你關於台灣的情形；有個朋友在地球另一邊，真是很好玩的事，我希望有一天能在臺灣見到你。

我和家人住在台北。我父親在一家外國銀行做會計，而我母親是一位教員。我有個姊姊在這裡一家公司當秘書。我就讀於一間很大的中學，是羅馬天主教神父所辦的。這個學校很不錯，很多學生畢業都進了大學。我也想進大學，不過在臺灣並不是想上大學的人都能上，因為學校沒有那麼多，所以要上大學很難。

* secondary school 中等學校；中學

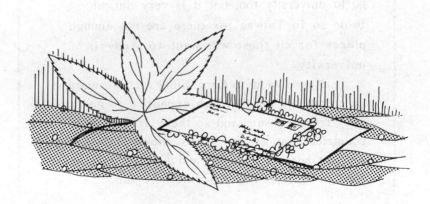

給筆友 (三)

（ Date ）

Dear Lydia,

It was lovely getting your letter two days ago. Thank you so much for it. You do seem to have had a good time on your holiday. I wish that I could have been with you. I was also very interested in what you have told me about your life and work in London.

I have also been on holiday. I was able to join some friends on a tour to the Philippines and we had a very good time there. We spent a few days in Manila, which is the capital, and then went to Baguio, a country town in the hills to the north of Manila. I usually save up as much money as I can in order to go away on holidays because Taiwan is very hot and sticky during the summer. I plan to go to Thailand next year and I hope that one day I will be able to save enough money to go to Europe.

Now I am back at work and am very busy in the office. My boss is an American and although he is kind, he always gives me a lot of work to do. I have been working for my boss since 2003 and I am very happy with the work.

Do please write again soon and I will also do so very soon.

With love,

....

　　*　　　很高興接到你前兩天的來信，謝謝你。你的假期似乎過得很愉快。

眞希望能跟你一起去，你說的倫敦的生活和工作，我覺得很有趣。

　　　　我也渡了假了，和幾個朋友到菲律賓旅行，玩得很愉快。我們在首

都馬尼拉玩了幾天，然後往馬尼拉北部的山間小鄉鎭碧瑤。由於台灣夏

天氣候又濕又熱，我總是儘量把錢省下來去渡假。我打算明年到泰國，

希望有一天有足夠的錢，能到歐洲去。

　　*　　　現在我又回來上班了，辦公室很忙碌。我的老板是美國人，人很好，

不過常給我一大堆工作做。我從一九八二年就開始爲他工作，工作滿愉

快的。

　　　　請儘量回信，我也會儘速回信。

*　***Baguio***〔ˈbægɪo〕*n.* 碧瑤（菲律賓的夏都，位於呂宋島西部）

　save up 貯錢

　sticky〔ˈstɪkɪ〕*adj.* 濕熱的

　Thailand〔ˈtaɪlənd〕*n.* 泰國

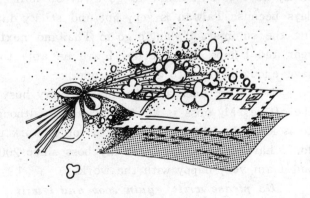

Ⅱ.佳節問候

　　佳節問候，一般人大都採用現成的賀卡，如果能在賀卡上加上親筆的問候語，將會讓人感到更親切。以下各例就是慶賀聖誕及新年的問候語。

恭賀聖誕

Dear Mike,

　　　　As we near the most joyous season of the year, we offer you our sincerest wishes for a very enjoyable holiday.

　　　　　　　　　　Sincerely,

　　　　　　　　　　.........

＊　　逢此佳節，我們誠摯的祝福你佳節愉快。

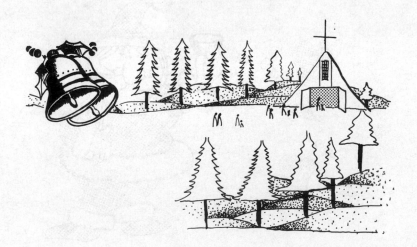

恭賀聖誕㈡

Dear Carol,

In the years which lie ahead may you realize great satisfaction and happiness in your
accomplishments. A Merry Christmas to you and
those dear children.

Sincerely,

....

* 願你在未來的一年，事事如意，樣樣稱心。謹祝你、鮑伯和那些親
愛的孩子們聖誕快樂。

恭賀聖誕㈢

Dear Steve,

As we once again approach the Christmas season, I should like to wish you a joyous holiday and express my hope for your happiness, and good fortune, in the years ahead.

Sincerely,

....

* 聖誕節又將來臨，謹祝你佳節愉快，並願你在未來的日子，快樂、幸運。

恭賀聖誕(四)

Dear Georgia and Gregory,

This year we promise again, as in the past, to drink a toast on Christmas Day to you both. The merriest of all Christmases to you and the hope that some day soon we shall be together.

Sincerely,

………

* 　和以往一樣，我們約定在聖誕節那天舉杯祝你們倆健康、佳節快樂，並希望我們很快能相聚。

賀 新 年

Dear Mike,

　　May this New Year be one that brings many good things your way.

　　　　　　　　　　　Sincerely,

　　　　　　　　　　　………

* 　　願新的這一年，帶給你許多美好的事物。

賀 新 年㈡

Dear Carol,

　　May you have a joyous holiday and may the New Year bring rich blessings for you and all those you love.

　　　　　　　　　　　Sincerely,

　　　　　　　　　　　………

* 　　祝你佳節愉快，並願這新的一年，你和所有你愛的人都幸福無比。

賀新年(三)

Dear Steve,

　　May your Holiday Season be a joyous one and may each day of the New Year bring you a full measure of success and happiness.

　　　　　　　　　Sincerely,

　　　　　　　　　.........

*　　祝你佳節愉快，並願新來的一年，每天你都無比成功、幸福。

賀 新 年㈣

Dear Georgia and Gregory,

It is with a warm feeling of friendship that I send you greetings of the season and my heartfelt best wishes. I hope that the beginning of the New Year will bring to you and yours a full measure of the blessings that make for happiness.

Sincerely,

....

* 帶著溫馨的友誼，我誠摯地祝福你佳節愉快，願新的一年帶給你們無比的幸福和快樂。

* heartfelt〔'hɑrt,fɛlt〕*adj.* 銘心的；至誠的

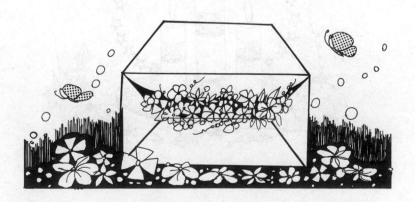

賀 新 年㈤

Dear Bess,

　　Rich blessings for health and abundant happiness is my wish for you in the coming year.

　　　　　　　　　　　Sincerely,

　　　　　　　　　　　.........

＊　　願你在未來的一年，身體健康，幸福、快樂。

第五章　慰問類

人們在病中或不如意時，格外需要他人的慰問和鼓勵，因此慰問信的
目的在表達溫馨友好的情誼，眞誠的了解、同情和鼓勵。

給病中的友人

February 26，2003

Dear Jane,

The Zonta Club just isn't the same without
you. So hurry up and beat that cold.

Have you heard the latest news about Ann
Hsia? She just announced her engagement to
David Chen. We're planning a surprise shower
and are looking forward to your being here.

All the members send their best wishes,
and we all hope to see you very soon.

Fondly,

....

---

* 　　崇她社不能沒有你，因此請快從感冒中康復吧！

　　　你聽說夏安最近的消息了嗎？她剛剛宣佈了和陳大衛訂婚的消息。

　　我們準備開一個令她驚喜的賀禮贈送會，希望你也能來參加。

　　　所有的社員都祝福你，並希望能早日見到你。

* 　shower〔ˈʃauə〕n.（爲卽將要出嫁及爲人母親而擧行的）賀禮贈送
會

給病中的友人㈡

March 2，2003

Dear Mr. Smith,

I was so sorry to hear you were in the hospital. *Do hurry and get well! Everyone at the office misses you and hopes you will be back at your desk very soon.*

Sincerely yours,

…………

給病中的友人㈢

March 10，2003

Dear Mrs. Hsia,

Mrs. Saunders and I are mighty sorry to hear of your illness. Your many friends here in Taipei are thinking of you and won't be happy until we hear you're completely recovered.

I understand you will be hospitalized for a few weeks, so I'm sending you the new best-seller to help you while away the time. I hope you will enjoy it.

Cordially yours,

…………

* mighty〔'maɪtɪ〕*adv*. 非常地
* while away the time 消磨時間
* I understand you will be … I hope you will enjoy it. 我知道你將住院數星期，因此送你新的暢銷書，幫助你消磨時間，希望你會喜歡它。

給病中的友人㈣

（Date）

Dear Jeff,

Sorry to hear about your illness. We were looking forward to that fishing trip which will have to be postponed, but only for a short time, I hope. Here's wishing you will be on your feet soon.

If there's something I can do to help you while away some time, please do let me know. Is there something you would like me to bring you when I come during visiting hours on Sunday?

The family have been asking about you and I have assured them that you will recover soon. Now, don't disappoint us.

Sincerely,

....

---

* to be on one's feet　復元
* Sorry to hear about your illness. ... Here's wishing you will be on your feet soon.　獲知你生病的消息，我很難過。原本盼望的釣魚旅行，只好延期了。不過，我希望不會延期太久。謹此祝你早日康復。
* disappoint〔͵dɪsə'pɔɪnt〕*vt.* 使失望

給將動手術的友人

（Date）

Dear Ann,

Alice called today to tell me that you have decided to have your operation immediately. If Dr. Wang tells you it is advisable, then it is sensible to have it over with once and for all. With all the modern facilities at Chang Gung Memorial Hospital, you should be up and about in a few weeks minus all the old aches and pains.

Hurry up and get well soon.

With best wishes,

Yours affectionately,

....

* 愛麗絲今天來訪，告訴我你決定立刻動手術，如果王醫師認爲適當的話，那麼這一勞永逸之擧，便是上策。長庚醫院擁有新式的設備，你幾星期後便可康復，再也沒有以往的疼痛了。

快康復吧！

祝福你

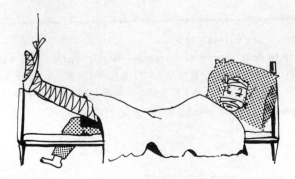

給生意失敗的友人

（Date）

Dear Mr. White,

My sympathy went with you when I learned of the unforeseen circumstances leading to the winding up of your business. Such an adverse turn in the business career of one who has achieved distinction as a successful merchant must be a hard blow. But as your ability and experience are well known in the business world, I am confident that many farsighted friends will soon help you start anew to retrieve your loss.

Yours sincerely,

....

* 　當我獲知你因爲預料不到的情況，而導致營業結束時，不禁同情。這種逆境，對一位成功的商人而言，必然是重大的打擊。但是你的才能與經驗，已聞名於商業界，我相信許多有遠見的朋友，不久將會幫助你東山再起，挽回損失。
* wind up　結束
* adverse〔əd'vɝs〕*adj.* 不利的
* farsighted〔'fɑr'saɪtɪd〕*adj.* 眼光遠大的
* retrieve〔rɪ'triv〕*vt.* 恢復

給未通過考試的友人

（Date）

Dear Stephen,

I was so sorry when your brother told me that you had not passed your final examination. I know how hard you have worked throughout the year and so you certainly deserved to pass. It seems so unfair that those who work so hard should not pass and so you have all my sympathy at this time.

I know how disappointed you must feel after all your effort, but the important thing is not to give up hope. I know that lots of famous people have failed examinations the first time and then later have done very well. I am sure that you will be like them and so I hope that you intend to try again next year and, with all the hard work you have done, I am sure that you will be successful next time. Please do not give up hope, but start to prepare for next time.

I send you my best wishes for your future.

Yours sincerely,

....

給未通過考試的友人㈡

（Date）

Dear Joe,

    I was sorry to learn that you had not been successful in the examination. Although I am sending you my sympathy, I feel you ought not to be unduly distressed at the result. You are still eligible to sit again for the examination and I am confident that this time next year, I shall be sending a letter, not of sympathy, but of congratulation.

    My kindest regards and best wishes,

Your sincere friend,

....

---

*　　獲知你未能通過考試，我感到難過。並衷心的同情你，但請不要太難過，你仍可參加下次的考試。而且我相信明年此時，我為你寫的是祝賀信，而不是慰問信。

　　祝福你。

*　eligible〔ˈɛlɪdʒəb!〕 *adj.* 合格的；合適的

*　sit for an examination　參加考試

給失戀的友人

（Date）

Dear Jack,

You must be now in the utmost distress after the recent frustration in love. But a failure in love is quite a common, though painful, thing. In your present state of mind, I know my words of consolation are futile. But time will not fail to heal your wound.

In fact if two hearts can not harmonize with each other, they cannot be really united into one. In such case, the earlier the severance, the happier for both parties. Don't lay the blame on her alone and be a good sport. I am sure you will find a new love before long.

Yours sincerely,

....

---

*　　在受過最近的戀愛挫折之後，現在你必定感到極端的難過。但失戀雖然痛苦，卻是極平常的事。我知道在你目前的心境下，安慰的話是無益的，但是時間將會治癒你的創傷。

事實上，兩心若不能和諧，是無法眞正結合爲一的。因此，在此情況下，愈早分離，對雙方愈好。不要只歸咎於她，做個開朗的人吧！我相信不久你就會找到新的伴侶了。

* frustration〔frʌs'treʃən〕*n.* 挫折

* futile〔'fjutḷ〕*adj.* 無益的

* heal〔hil〕*vt.* 使復原

* harmonize〔'hɑrmə͵naɪz〕*vi.* 和諧

* severance〔'sɛvərəns〕*n.* 分離

* sport〔sport, spɔrt〕*n.* 明朗的人

給去職的友人

（Date）

Dear Mr. Hsia,

I was astonished when I learned that you had lost your position. Please don't feel too much distressed by this frustration. A well-educated and competent young man like you cannot be laid off too long, and I am sure you will soon get an even better position.

Please let me know of any assistance I can render to you.

Sincerely,

††††††††††††

---

* 　獲知你失去職位，我感到很驚異。請不要爲這個挫折太難過。像你這般受過良好教育又能幹的青年，是不會賦閒太久的，我相信不久你將會獲得更好的職位。

　任何需要我幫忙之處，請告訴我。

* competent 〔ˊkɑmpətənt〕 *adj*. 能幹的

* lay off 暫時解雇

* render 〔ˊrɛndɚ〕 *vt*. 給與

第六章　弔唁類

　　寫弔唁信只有一個目的，就是要給遺屬安慰。因此弔唁信難寫，然而卻最需要寫。

　　在得知喪聞後，要儘早寫弔唁信。信文應簡短、眞誠、有技巧，表達同情或對死者的仰慕、懷念等。但要避免虛情，及引起悲傷的字句，如「悲慘」、「絕望」等。

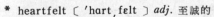

一般通用弔唁函

May 20，2003

Dear Amy,

　　　There is little one can say at a time like this.　But I'd like you to know that I'm thinking of you and that you have my heartfelt sympathy.

　　　　　　　Sincerely,

　　　　　　　…………

*　　　在這個時候，實在很難表達要說的話。但我願你知道，我想念著你，並對你衷心的同情。

* heartfelt 〔 'hɑrt͵fɛlt 〕 *adj.* 至誠的

唁友喪父

March 3, 2003

Dear Mary,

Your father had a rich, full life and lived every minute of it without regrets. Let the thoughts of a life well-spent be your consolation now. Knowing your father as I did, I am sure that is the way he would have wanted it.

You will miss him, as we all will. But time will bring comfort in the fond memories of your many good years together.

George and the boys join me in sending our deepest sympathy.

Affectionately,

....

---

*　　令尊擁有美滿充實的一生，毫無遺憾的度過每個時刻。就讓「他一生都過得很圓滿」的想法，作爲你的慰藉吧。我知道令尊的爲人，因此相信他必定也希望你這樣做。

你會懷念他，就如我們都會懷念他一樣。但記憶中，共同度過的多年的美好歲月，將會帶來慰藉。

喬治、孩子們與我一起向你致最深的同情。

唁友喪母

(Date)

Dear Betty,

    I will just write this short note to say how deeply grieved I was to hear the news of your dear mother's death. The shock to all of you must have been terrible. May God sustain you in your sore trial. It must be a great comfort to you to know how ready your mother was for the call to a better world. No more saintly or charitable woman ever lived. If I can be of any help, do not hesitate to let me hear.

        Yours affectionately,

....

* sustain〔sə'sten〕 *vt.* 支持
  sore〔sor〕 *adj.* 使人痛苦的
  charitable〔'tʃærətəbl〕 *adj.* 仁慈的

唁友喪夫

April 30, 2003

Dear Alice,

I know how little the words and acts of friends can do to ease the grief that has come to you. The death of a loved one is always hard to bear, and I can imagine the terrible void left by Jack. *He was such a vital, gay person and such a good one.*

I want you to know how often I have thought of you and how deeply I sympathize with you in your bereavement.

Sincerely,

....

* void〔vɔɪd〕*n.* 空虛
* vital〔'vaɪtḷ〕*adj.* 充滿生命力的
* bereavement〔bə'rivmənt〕*n.* 傷慟（親人之死亡）

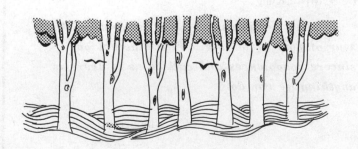

唁友喪夫㈡

（Date）

Dear Julia,

The sudden passing of Bill was a great shock to all of us. We will all miss him but he will live on for us, as he must for you, in happy memories.

Please , Julia dear, call upon me for any service I can render. In this sad hour, my heart is with you.

Affectionately,

....

* live on   繼續活著
* We will all miss him … memories.   我們都會想念他，他將活在你和我們快樂的記憶中。

唁友喪夫㈢

（Date）

Dear Mrs. Kung,

Mrs. Tompkins and I are *deeply sorry to hear of your great loss. Please accept our sincere condolences and call on us if there is anything we can do.*

Sincerely,

....

唁友喪夫㈣

(Date)

Dear Mrs. Jones,

My heart is heavy at the sad news of the death of your devoted husband. He was a splendid man, brilliant, an upright leader in the community and an outstanding citizen.

The community and his many friends will miss him.

With deep sympathy,

Sincerely yours,

....

唁友喪妻

(Date)

Dear Mr. Forbes,

May I extend to you my sincere sympathy at your loss.

Although I never had the privilege of knowing Harriet, I know how deeply you must be affected.

Please accept my heartfelt condolences in this hour of sorrow.

Very sincerely,

....

唁友喪妻 (二)

(Date)

Dear Mr. Carter,

The officers of Community Activities express their grief over the untimely death of your beloved wife who served as chairman of the Fund Raising Committee. She gave unstintingly of herself as a leader of women and devoted her life to the cause of philanthropy. The example of her courage will remain as a source of continued inspiration to all of us.

To you, her family, and her many friends, we extend our heartfelt sympathy.

Sincerely,

....

* unstintingly 〔ʌn'stɪntɪŋlɪ〕 *adv*. 不吝惜地
* cause 〔kɔz〕 *n*. 理想
* philanthropy 〔fə'lænθrəpɪ〕 *n*. 慈善事業
* inspiration 〔͵ɪnspə'reʃən〕 *n*. 激勵之事物
* She gave unstintingly … philanthropy. 她全心全力的做為婦女的領導者，並為慈善事業的目標，奉獻一生。

唁友喪子

(Date)

Dear Rosa and Fred,

There are no words that can express our great sorrow at the loss of your son. We loved Dick very much and our heartfelt sympathy goes out to you.

Ben feels that it might be best for you to join us this summer at Skytop. I think you will find the peace and quiet of the country restful and soothing.

Please accept our sincere condolences.

Very cordially,

....

* restful 〔 ′rɛstfəl 〕 *adj.* 恬靜的
* soothing 〔 ′suðɪŋ 〕 *adj.* 安慰的

第七章 致謝類

① 收到慶賀信、慰問信或接受款待、幫忙後，應儘早函謝。

② 語氣要眞誠。

③ 應親筆回謝函。

I．謝祝賀

謝賀訂婚

March 22, 2003

Dear Tom,

The bliss of our engagement would not seem complete without the thoughtful letter you sent us. Thank you for your sharing the joy of your friends, and for the warmest sentiments which I know come from the heart.

As ever,

....

謝賀結婚

February 16, 2003

Dear Susan,

There is nothing more important to us than to receive your letter. We are very grateful for your congratulations and good wishes.

With our renewed thanks for your kindness,

Sincerely,

....

謝贈結婚禮物

January 22, 2003

Dear Mrs. Brown,

Thank you and Mr. Thomas so very much for the lovely silver bowl. Jack and I will certainly enjoy using it in our new home.

With deep appreciation,

Sincerely,

....

* silver bowl 銀碗

謝賀生日

（Date）

Dear Nancy,

It was thoughtful of you to remember my birthday. I really appreciate your good wishes and great letter. I can't recall when I've received such a touching message.

It was good hearing from you again. Mother joins me in sending our warmest regards to you.

As ever,

....

* touching〔'tʌtʃɪŋ〕 *adj*. 動人的
* regards〔rɪ'gɑrdz〕 *n*. 問候

謝贈生日禮物

（Date）

Dear Nancy,

I cannot tell you how delighted I was with the handsome birthday present you gave me. It really is a most wonderful gift which I shall always treasure.

Please accept my thanks not only for the beautiful gift but also for the good wishes which you kindly sent with it.

Your affectionate friend,

....

謝賀畢業

（Date）

Dear Tom,

One of the best things about graduation was getting so many nice letters from my friends.

Thank you ever so much for your congratulations and good wishes. I hope I can live up to them.

My best wishes to all your family,

Cordially,

....

* live up to 實行

謝賀升遷

（Date）

Dear Chen,

  It's very kind of you to write. ***Thank you so much for your congratulations and good wishes***. I fear I do not deserve it.

  This promotion brings me mixed feelings of joy and dread. It's a joy to know there is someone to appreciate what I've done, and the dread that my inexperience will do blunders.

  Thank you once again.

        As ever,

        ....

* blunder〔'blʌndɚ〕*n.* 愚蠢的錯誤

謝贈聖誕禮物

（Date）

Dear George,

  What a wonderful Christmas present you sent me！ You certainly know my taste and my insatiable appetite for beautiful things.

  Thanks so much, George. It was very thoughtful of you to remember me, and I really do appreciate it.

       Yours sincerely,

       ....

* insatiable〔ɪn'seʃɪəbl̩〕*adj.* 不知足的

Ⅱ.謝款待

謝　款　待

（Date）

Dear Mrs. White,

 Thank you so much for the marvelous weekend at Green Island. I can't remember when I have had a more pleasant or relaxing time.

 It was most thoughtful of you and Mr. March to invite me, and I warmly appreciate your hospitality.

        Sincerely,

        …………

謝　款　待 ㈡

（Date）

Dear Janet,

 What a lovely evening we spent with you and Ed, *and how nice to see you both looking so well.*

 We enjoyed everything-congenial company, delicious dinner, good bridge game.

 We hope the new house will be a source of happiness to you both, and we look forward to seeing you when you recover from the excitement of moving.

        Affectionately,

        …………

---

* congenial 〔 kən'dʒinjəl 〕 *adj.* 意氣相投的

* emerge 〔 ɪ'mɝdʒ 〕 *vi.* 出現

謝 款 待 (三)

（Date）

Dear Mrs. Lin,

I would like to thank you very much for the most enjoyable evening I had with you last night. It was very kind of you to invite me to dinner and I thoroughly enjoyed myself.

I was very pleased to meet both you and your husband again and I found what you told me about life in London very interesting. It was also a great pleasure to meet your other friends and I know that I shall take very happy memories of your party back with me to Taipei.

I hope that you will soon be able to visit Taipei again and then I look forward to returning your hospitality.

With my very best wishes to both you and your husband,

Yours sincerely,

....

謝 款 待㈣

（Date）

Dear George,

　　I have come away from the convention greatly impressed with the cordiality of your officers and members and their wonderful hospitality.　I was made to feel during my stay that I belong with you.　Most impressive was the way in which I was bade farewell.　I was made to feel that I was leaving only to return in a short time.

　　It was an experience I am not likely to forget.　Thank you and all your officers and members for making my stay with you so very pleasurable.

　　　　　　　　　Sincerely,

　　　　　　　　　…………

* cordiality〔kɔr′dʒælətɪ〕 *n.* 友善；誠懇
* bid ～ farewell　告別（被動詞態爲～ be bade farewell）

謝 款 待㈤

（Date）

Dear Janet,

　　We are still enjoying our visit with you, in retrospect. Every minute was perfect, and even the wretched trip home failed to dampen our enthusiasm.

　　Again, *we thank you for hospitality that made us feel as comfortable as we do in our own home*; for unsurpassed companionship; for tender, loving care; for gifts; for everything.

　　　　　　　　　Sincerely,

　　　　　　　　　‥‥‥‥‥

* retrospect 〔'rɛtrə,spɛkt 〕 *n.* 回顧；追憶
* wretched 〔'rɛtʃɪd 〕 *adj.* 可憐的；悲悽的
* dampen 〔'dæmpən 〕 *vt.* 減弱
* unsurpassed 〔,ʌnsə'pæst 〕 *adj.* 最優的

謝　款　待㈥

（Date）

Dear John,

　　　　You couldn't have done a nicer thing than
to arrange that wonderful luncheon at the
Hamilton Hotel for me.　I so enjoyed having a
chat with you and the others, and it is just the
thing I think of when I'm nostalgic for home.
I do hope I'll see you in Long Island one of
these days.

　　　　Thank you again for being so thoughtful,
as you always have been and always are.

　　　　　　　　　　　　Sincerely,

　　　　　　　　　　　　…………

* You couldn't have done … for me.　你爲我在漢米敦旅舘安排的午
　餐眞是太美好了。
* chat 〔 tʃæt 〕 n. 閒談
* nostalgic 〔 nɑˊstældʒık 〕 adj. 思鄉病的

Ⅲ. 謝幫助

謝 幫 助

（Date）

Dear Sir,

Many thanks for the favour you did for me, and the kind interest you took in me. I am glad to inform you that by your invaluable recommendation, I have obtained the position I applied for.

I shall exert my best efforts in performing my duties, and try to be worthy of your assistance.

My best regards,

Yours respectfully,

....

* interest 〔 ˈɪntrɪst 〕 *n.* 關心
* invaluable 〔 ɪnˈvæljəbḷ 〕 *adj.* 無價的
* exert one's best efforts 盡最大的努力
* perform one's duties 盡責任

謝幫助 ⊜

（Date）

Dear Dr. Robinson,

It was very considerate of you to take the time to write to the Dean of Admissions of Hope University concerning my qualifications and background.

If I am fortunate enough to be accepted, I'll do my best to live up to the good things you said about me.

I very much appreciate what you did.

Gratefully,

....

謝幫助 ⊜

（Date）

Dear Alice,

There may be some other very thoughtful people who would think of sending that nice letter to us, but very few who would actually follow up the thought with action. Thank you so very much for Dana and me. We hope we will see you and Raymond soon, and in the meantime we send our very best regards.

Affectionately,

....

謝金錢援助

(Date)

Dear Jim,

A friend in need is a friend indeed. That was what I felt when you promptly answered my request for financial assistance at a very critical moment. Though you well knew how reluctantly I put my difficulties before you, I was still afraid that I might be guilty of causing you too much inconvenience in letting me have the sum I so badly needed.

Please accept my most cordial thanks for your timely help which will be engraved in my thankful mind.

Yours gratefully,

....

---

* critical moment　重要關頭；危機
* badly〔 ′bædlɪ 〕 *adv*. 非常地

謝幫助慈善義賣

（Date）

Dear Mrs. Blakely,

I wish there were a better word than "thanks" to express my appreciation for your generous help in making the Charity Bazaar a success.

Thanks for giving me the thrill of bringing your wonderful work to the attention of the trustees at our next meeting.

All my best wishes.

Sincerely

....

* charity Bazaar 慈善義賣
* trustee 〔trʌs'ti〕 *n.* 董事

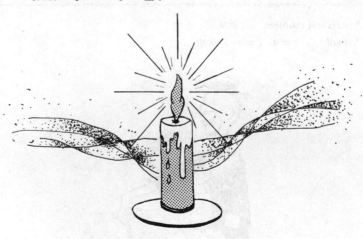

Ⅳ.謝慰問

謝 探 病

（Date）

Dear Mr. Liu,

Thanks for your kind visit which has made me forget my illness, and strange to say, the doctor told me this afternoon that my condition has suddenly improved a great deal. It is all owing to your friendship, I should say.

The doctor assured me if such improvement continued I should be able to leave the sick-bed within a few days. You can imagine how the news has cheered me up.

Sincerely yours,

....

謝 送 花

(Date)

Dear George,

    Now that I am able to write again, *I want to thank you for the lovely flowers. They helped cheer me up on several gloomy days, not only because they added color to the room but because they reminded me of a good friend's thoughtfulness.*

    I hope I shall soon be able to call on you.

                      Yours sincerely,

                      ....

謝 慰 問

(Date)

Dear Mr. Wu,

    Thank you for your kind expression of sympathy. My family and I shall always appreciate your thoughtfulness.

                      Yours sincerely,

                      ....

V. 謝弔唁

謝 弔 唁

（Date）

Emily dear,

Your letter brought me great comfort. *I truly appreciate your sympathy and understanding, and above all, your offer of help.* Your kind expression of sympathy helped me a lot, and it is much appreciated.

Thanks so much for writing.

Affectionately yours,

....

謝 弔 唁 （二）

（Date）

Dear Mr. Lin,

We deeply appreciate the way our friends rallied around when we needed them. *Your sympathetic and diligent assistance will long be remembered.*

Sincerely,

....

* rally around （爲援助、激勵而）集合

謝唁喪父

（Date）

Dear Rosa,

I want you to know how very much your thoughtfulness at the time of Father's death has meant to me. Your sympathy and kindness will always be remembered.

Affectionately

....

謝唁喪父㈡

（Date）

Dear Mrs. Blakely,

How kind of you to write me that wonderful letter. It is comforting to know that Dad had such fine associates, and that he will be remembered by those with whom he worked for so long.

Sincerely yours,

....

* associate 〔ə'soʃɪɪt〕 n.同事

謝唁喪父(三)

（Date）

Dear Mrs. Watson,

　　Mother is making a valiant effort to rally after Dad's death, but she is not yet up to writing letters.　She greatly appreciated your message of sympathy and has asked me to thank you.

　　　　　　　　　　　　Sincerely yours,

　　　　　　　　　　　　..............

---

* valiant 〔 ˈvæljənt 〕 *adj.* 勇敢的
* rally 〔ˈrælɪ 〕 *vi.* 恢復（精神、體力）

謝唁喪母

（Date）

Dear Mr. Horton,

　　Thank you very much for your condolence with me on the loss of my Mother.　*I shall try to be courageous by thinking of your sympathy.*

　　　　　　　　　　　　Yours truly,

　　　　　　　　　　　　.............

---

* condolence 〔ˈkɑndələns 〕 *n.* 弔慰

謝唁喪母 (二)

(Date)

Dear Mrs. Jameson,

We all deeply appreciate your most kind letter. Our grief is indeed most bitter. Mother was everything to us. She never had a thought for herself, and spent her whole life thinking how best she could make us happy. Everybody I have spoken to seems to have loved and respected her. Well, we have got to face our loss as we know she would have wished us to face it. Thank you so much for your kind offer of help.

Sincerely,

....

* Mother was everything to us. 對我們而言，母親重於一切。

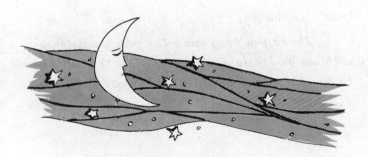

謝醫生

（Date）

Dear Dr. Wang,

On behalf of my mother and the rest of the family, may I be allowed to thank you for all the kind attention that you gave my father during his long illness. We all realize that you did everything that lay in your power to relieve him of pain and to comfort him.

You will like to know that he always spoke in the kindest terms of your visits. We are all most grateful to you for your sympathy and your help.

Our kindest regards,

Yours very truly,

....

* *on behalf of* ～ 代表～
* *in one's power* 在某人的能力範圍之內

Thank you, doctor!

第八章 道歉類

有時候我們不免因為過失或疏忽，須向別人道歉，這種情況下，道歉函要立刻寫。若因不得已的原因而犯錯，則不妨加以解釋，但不要強辯，以免引起人家的反感；如果是自己的疏忽，則應坦承無諱，並表明以後不再犯，必要的話，應設法補救。

犯錯道歉

（ Date ）

Dear John,

    I'm writing to apologize for my poor behavior at your party last night. I know my behavior was inexcusable and undeserving of forgiveness. I am very, very sorry for the embarrassment I caused. I shall try not to be so rude again.

                   Sincerely yours,

                   ....

---

* behavior〔bɪˈhevjə〕n. 行為
* inexcusable〔ˌɪnɪkˈskjuzəbl̩〕adj. 不能原諒的
* undeserving〔ˌʌndɪˈzɝvɪŋ〕adj. 不配的
* embarrassment〔ɪmˈbærəsmənt〕n. 困窘

弄壞物品道歉

（Date ）

Dear Mrs. White,

　　The first thing I did this morning was to telephone the best rug weaver in the city. He has assured me that he can repair the burn I so carelessly made in your beautiful rug yesterday.

　　Mr. Chen will call you tomorrow and arrange to see the rug and match the color. The bill will be sent to me, of course.

　　It was so nice of you to make so little of the accident. My carelessness was unforgivable.

　　　　Sincerely,

　　　　…………

* rug 〔rʌg〕 *n.* 地毯
* weaver 〔'wivə〕 *n.* 織工
* *make little of* 不重視

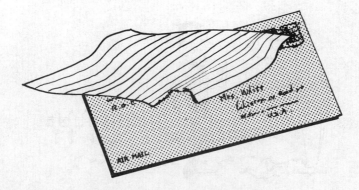

爲狗弄壞別人的花園道歉

（Date）

My dear Mrs. Lu,

Unfortunately, our dog Rover has been scratching in your garden and has ruined your pretty pansies. I am so sorry. We have asked the Bacon Greenhouse to supply you with new plants, and they will be phoning to take your order tomorrow. We have long talked of enclosing our lawn with a fence, and at last we have that ordered, too! Meanwhile, I'll keep Rover tied up and see that he buries his bones in his own yard.

Sincerely yours,

....

* scratch〔skrætʃ〕*vi.* 抓
* pansy〔'pænzɪ〕*n.* 三色紫羅蘭
* greenhouse〔'grin‚haʊs〕*n.* 花房
* enclose〔ɪn'kloz〕*vt.*（用籬笆、牆等）圍起來

打破玻璃道歉

（Date）

My dear Mrs. Chuang,

　　I find that Dick has broken a window in your basement. Maybe all little boys have to find out that balls can break glass, but I am sorry it was your window and not ours that he used for his experiment. Mr. Wu, phone 2701-3232, does repair work for us. If you will let him know when it would be convenient for you to have a new pane put in, he will replace the glass and charge the amount to us.

　　　　　　　　　　　Very truly yours,

　　　　　　　　　　　.....................

---

* 　　我發現狄克打破了你地下室的窗子。或許所有的小孩子都得發現球
會打破玻璃；不過，很遺憾他的實驗是用你的玻璃，而不是我們的。吳
先生幫我們修玻璃，他的電話是 2701-3232。如果你能通知他，幾時去修
理玻璃對您較方便，他就會去修，然後再向我們收取費用。

* pane〔pen〕*n*. 門窗上之單塊的玻璃

* charge〔tʃɑrdʒ〕*vt*. 記帳

打破車窗玻璃道歉

（Date）

Dear Mr. Wang,

    Peter has explained to us the unfortunate incident of your windshield's being directly in the path of his baseball. He wanted to go immediately and apologize himself, but didn't quite know how to go about it.

    I have checked with Chung Shan Garage, and they tell me it will cost $ 5,000 to replace the glass. Peter has agreed to pay for this out of his allowance, and I am advancing this sum to him with the enclosed check.

    We are sincerely sorry that it occurred and I know that all the boys will be more careful in the future.

Very sincerely yours,

....

* 彼得跟我們解釋過，他打棒球時，球不巧打中您的擋風玻璃。他原想立刻向您道歉，卻又不知道該怎麼做才好。

    我問過中山汽車修理廠，他們告訴我，換這種玻璃要五千元，彼得答應由他的零用錢來償付。現在我隨函附上支票，先代他墊這筆款項。

    我們很抱歉發生這種事，我確信孩子們以後會更加小心的。

* windshield〔'wɪnd‚ʃild〕*n*.（汽車之）擋風玻璃
* *go about* 著手；忙於
* garage〔gə'rɑʒ, gə'rɑdʒ〕*n*. 車庫；修車廠
* allowance〔ə'lauəns〕*n*. 零用錢

為遺失所借物品道歉

(Date)

Dear Henry,

I am sorry to tell you that I am unable to return the book that you were kind enough to lend me last month.

I finished the book last week, and intended to return it to you today as I had promised to do. Yesterday I was unable to find it in the bookcase where it should have been. Obviously someone has taken it away without first letting me know.

I am still trying to locate the book. In case I cannot find it in the next few days, I shall get a new one for you. I fully realize that old books are like old friends, and a new book cannot take the place of an old one.

Even if I finally recover the book, my delay in returning it to you will certainly have caused you some inconvience. Again, I apologize for not returning the book.

Yours sincerely,

....

---

* bookcase 〔'bʊk͵kes〕 *n.* 書架
*   Yesterday I was unable to find it in … Obviously someone had taken it away without first letting me know. 昨天我在書架上原來放的地方找不到它。顯然有人沒事先徵得我同意，就把它拿走。
* locate 〔'loket, lo'ket〕 *vt.* 尋出～的位置

爲遲延還書道歉

（Date）

Dear Mr. Wang,

　　I'm so sorry for not returning your book, *Zen and the Art of Motorcycle Maintenance*, to you sooner. After I had finished reading it, several in my family decided to read it, too. Then a friend of mine, Mr. Chen, was so intrigued by the book's title that he asked me to allow him to read it, so I'm afraid I have borrowed the book from you longer than expected.

　　　　　　　　　　　　Sincerely yours,

　　　　　　　　　　　　·················

* Zen〔zɛn〕*n*. （佛教中之）禪宗
* maintenance〔'mentənəns, -tɪnəns〕*n*. 保養
* intrigue〔ɪn'trig〕*vt*. 激起興趣；吸引

爲喧鬧道歉

（Date）

Dear Mrs. Lin,

The superintendent informed us that you were annoyed by our television last night. We certainly do not want to cause you any disturbance, particularly in view of Mr. Lin's condition. If you had called the matter to our attention immediately, we would have lowered the volume and closed the windows.

The boys are extremely interested in night baseball games, and I am sorry that their noise bothered you and I hope that it won't happen again.

If at any time you should find our activities bothersome, please do not hesitate to let us know. We shall try to cooperate in every way we can.

Sincerely yours,

....

---

* 　管理員通知我們，你昨夜被我家的電視聲音吵到。我們當然不希望引起你的困擾，尤其林先生在這種狀況下。如果你那時能立刻通知我們，我們就會把聲音關小並關上窗戶。
　　孩子們喜歡看夜間棒球賽，我很抱歉他們的叫鬧聲吵到你，我想這種事不會再發生了。

* superintendent〔͵suprɪn'tɛndənt〕*n.* 管理者；指揮者
* disturbance〔dɪ'stɝbəns〕*n.* 擾亂；騷動
* in view of ~　由於～緣故；鑒於～
* bothersome〔'bɑðəsəm〕*adj.* 惹起麻煩的；惹人煩惱的

爲不能赴約道歉

(Date)

Dear Mrs. Wang,

I do apologize for having to send you the telegram about Monday night.

When I accepted your invitation, I stupidly forgot that Monday was a holiday and that my own guests, naturally, were not leaving until Tuesday morning; Joseph and I could not very well go out by ourselves and leave them!

We were disappointed and hope that you know how sorry we were not to be with you.

Very sincerely,

....

* When I accepted ⋯ go out by ourselves and leave them! 接受你的邀請時，我眞胡塗，因爲我忘了星期一放假，而我家的客人要到星期二早上才會離開。約瑟夫和我總不好自己出門，而把客人留在家裏。

失約道歉

（Date ）

Dear Mr. Chen,

　　I am writing to apologize for missing my appointment yesterday afternoon. I am afraid I was not well and I was unable to phone to cancel the appointment.

　　If it is possible I would like to make another appointment for the same time next week.

　　　　　　　　　　　　Yours sincerely,

　　　　　　　　　　　　………………

失約道歉㈡

(Date)

Dear Ann,

    I'm sorry I missed seeing you yesterday. I know that you must have been disappointed in not seeing the play. The fact is, my boss, at the last moment, gave me some urgent work to do and I couldn't get to a phone to call you. I'm terribly sorry.

    I would, however, like to ask you out this weekend to make up for yesterday. I hope that you would still like to see me. I am waiting for your reply.

                    Yours,

                    ....

*   很抱歉昨天沒能和你碰面。我想那齣戲你看不成，一定很失望。實在是因我的老板臨下班前，才交給我一些急事處理，而我又不能給你電話，眞是抱歉。

    不管如何，這個週末我想邀你出去，補償昨天的過失。我希望你還願意見我，謹候你的答覆。

失約道歉㈢

(Date)

Dear Cathy,

Will you forgive me for not having met you for lunch while I was in Taichung? I had planned to call you in the morning at the office, but an unexpected client conference tied me up until it was time to rush for the plane.

I expect to be in the city again next month, and will call you a couple of days in advance — and this time, I promise to make it.

Yours very truly,

....

* 你能原諒我到台中來時，沒有和你共進午餐嗎？那天早上在辦公室時，本想打電話給你，卻突然開了一個客戶會議，使我忙到臨上飛機前。

下個月我將再來一次，前幾天就會通知你，而且這次我保證言出必行。

* *be tied up* 非常忙碌

失約道歉㈣

（Date ）

Dear Henry,

　　　You are entitled to give me thirty lashes. I did expect to visit you and Winnie, but the family was more demanding than I had expected, and it wasn't until we got back home that I realized I didn't even have a chance to call you and say hello.

　　　　　　　　　　　　Sincerely yours,

　　　　　　　　　　　　..................

* *entitle to～*　有資格做～；有做～的權利
* lash〔læʃ〕*n.* 鞭打

失約道歉(五)

（Date ）

My dear Vicky,

I am terribly sorry I couldn't get to the club this afternoon. I would have called you, but I was hunting frantically for little Mike for almost two hours. He was out in the yard at noon and just vanished. Mrs. Chen, our sitter, and I combed the neighborhood calling him and getting more and more frightened.

When I decided to go home and call the police, didn't I find my precious sound asleep on his blanket in his *closet*! Of course, then he woke up hungry and furious, and it was too late for the club.

Please forgive us, Vicky, and come here next week, for I believe it's my turn to entertain.

Most contritely,

....

---

* frantically〔'fræntɪkl̩ɪ〕*adv.* 瘋狂似地；狂亂地

* comb〔kom〕*vt.* 到處搜尋

* contritely〔kən'traɪtlɪ〕*adv.* 悔悟地；懺悔地

* entertain〔͵ɛntə'ten〕*vt.* 款待；招待

第九章 情書類

寫情書只有一個原則，就是要發自內心；要自然、誠懇，表現自己的風格。

I.第一次約會

以下由於是初交往，因此一往一答中，彼此稱呼和署名都較客氣。

第一次約會

(Date)

Dear Miss Liu,

　　I hope it will not appear impertinent to write you this letter after we have met but for the first time. The fact is, I am most anxious to know you better, and I venture to ask you to do me a favour. May I ask you for a date on Saturday evening, May 12 th ?

　　As you know, our school is having its annual dinner dance on that day. Each of the students attending the dance is bringing a partner. *As I have known no other girls except you, and even if I had many girl friends you are the only girl I would care to go to a ball with, so won't you kindly give a nod to say yes*?

　　Until your reply comes——and I am hoping it is a beaming, Yes——my heart and my mind won't have a moment's peace.

Yours sincerely,

．．．．．．．．．．．．．．．．

*　　　僅僅見過一面，就寫信給你，希望不至於太唐突，實在是因爲我很想多了解你，並斗膽請你幫個忙，請問我能在五月十二日週末夜邀約你嗎？

　　　如你所知，當天我們學校將舉行一年一度的晚宴舞會，每個到場的同學都需帶一位舞伴。除了你以外，我不認識其他的女孩子，而且即使我有其他的女朋友，你也是我想帶去舞會的唯一的女孩子，你能不能行行好，點個頭答應我呢？

　　　在你的答覆到來前——哦，希望是令人愉快的，我的心將一刻也不能安寧。

*　appear impertinent　顯得唐突
*　*venture to*　斗膽；膽敢
*　beaming〔'bimɪŋ〕*adj.*愉快的

答 覆

（Date）

Dear Mr. Chuang,

It is most charming of you to write and ask me to be your dancing partner at our school's annual ball. I am glad to accept your suggestion.

Please tell me what time you are going to pick me up, and I shall be ready.

Yours cordially,

....

* 　很高興收到你的信，並邀我做你的舞伴，參加學校一年一度的舞會，我很樂意接受你的邀請。

　　請告訴我幾時來接我，我將會準備好等你。

II.男女朋友信件

給 女 友

（Date）

My darling Cathy,

    I arrived here last night and found all the family in the best of health and spirits. Everyone enquired very kindly after you. It is pouring rain this morning, so I thought I would just stay indoors and write you a letter. The others have gone for a walk along the shore. I'm afraid they will get drenched to the skin. I hope you got home quite safely yesterday. I can tell you, I wished all the journey you had been with me, and I am looking forward more than I can say to seeing you again. I suppose I shall hear from you today or tomorrow, and that is the next best thing. What did you do last night? I am beginning to hate this place for parting us even for a week. It will seem like an age. Have you started reading the book I gave you? Dear Cathy, how I wish you were here. Is your Aunt better today? If you are not here, at any rate your photograph is. I am looking at it at this moment.

        Much love from,

        Neil

* *enquire after*　問候；問安
* drench〔drɛntʃ〕*vt.* 浸；浸透
* *drench to the skin*　渾身濕透
* *at any rate*　無論如何

給 男 友

(Date)

My darling Neil,

I was so glad to get your letter and hear all your news — though I'm afraid it was mostly news about myself! What a dear old thing you are! I felt very down in the dumps when I left you on Tuesday morning at the station. I took a taxi home, which was very extravagant ; but it was raining so heavily. Indeed it is still, so we are no better off here than you are. Auntie seems better today. It seems such an age since you left. I hope you got the little note I wrote last night. I'm going to write you a long letter tomorrow, and I shall expect one from you on Saturday! I've begun to read the book. Does *Ellen* marry him? I feel so tempted to read the end part first! Give my love to all your family. Auntie sends you her love, and asks me to say that she thinks I am missing you very much! Did you ever hear such a thing! — but I am.

Your most loving,
Cathy

* I felt very down in the dumps when…, I'm going to write you a long letter tomorrow, 星期二早上自車站離開你以後，覺得意氣很消沈。我坐計程車回家，眞是奢侈！不過雨實在下得很大，事實上現在仍在下，因此我們這裡並不比你那裡好。姑媽今天看來好多了。自你離開後，眞覺得有一整年之久了呢！希望你已收到我昨夜寫給你的小卡片，明天我要給你寫封很長很長的信。

* I feel very down in the dumps. 我覺得意氣很消沈。

* extravagant 〔ɪkˈstrævəgənt〕 *adj.* 奢侈的；浪費的

Ⅲ. 求婚信

求 婚

(Date)

Dear Liz,

For a long time I have wanted to ask you a question of the deepest importance to myself. Can you guess what it is? You know what friends we have been for years, and how much we have seen one another. Well, Liz, the more I have seen of you the more certain I am that all my future happiness lies in your hands. Before meeting you yesterday I had determined to ask you to be my wife, but when the moment came I found that I was tongue-tied and could not say a single word. But I ask you now. Will you be my wife? Dear Liz, I love you more than everything in the world. I could cover sheets of paper and yet not say half that I feel, but what would be the good of it? The one question covers everything else. I eagerly await your answer. If it is "yes" I shall be the happiest person in the world; if it is "no" I shall try and bear it like a man.

From

Ted

* *see one another* （男女）彼此約會
* tongue‐tied〔'tʌŋ,taɪd〕*adj.* 張口結舌的；說不出話的
* cover sheets of paper 寫滿好幾頁紙

答 覆

(Date)

Dear Ted,

　　I received your letter last night and have read it over and over again. It has made me un-utterably happy. Yes, Ted, that's my answer. I feel like the proudest girl on earth. I don't think I slept a wink all night. Do you know, I wondered why you were so silent last time we met. How little I guessed the real cause! It seems all too wonderful to be true. I feel as if it must be a lovely dream. Come round this evening and see,

　　　　　　　　　　Your own,

　　　　　　　　　　Liz

* unutterably〔ʌn'ʌtərəblɪ〕*adv.* 不可言喩地

拒　絕

(Date)

Dear John,

　　I was most surprised to receive your letter yesterday. It is true that we have known each other since we have been children together, but it was never in my mind, as apparently it has been in yours, that there existed anything more than a friendship between us. Your unkind suggestion that I have jilted you is both unjust and baseless.

　　I think you will agree that there has been nothing in my conduct to lead you or anyone else to suppppose that I felt for you other than as a friend. I never dreamed that you entertained for me the feeling that you now profess.

　　I hope that we both, you and I, can destroy and forget this correspondence.

　　　　　　　　　　　Yours sincerely,

　　　　　　　　　　　....................

* jilt〔dʒɪlt〕*vt.* 遺棄；拋棄（情人）
* *feel for* ～　對～有感情

給情人的父親的求婚信

（ Date ）

Dear sir,

I feel that the time has come for me to tell you what you must have suspected for some months, that I am in love with your daughter Lisa. I have her permission also to say that she is in love with me.

I am now writing formally to ask for your consent to our being engaged to be married. I should be delighted to have an opportunity of discussing my future business prospects with you, as I believe I am in a position to give Lisa a comfortable little home.

If you give your permission to our engagement, as we both greatly hope, I promise to do all in my power to make Lisa happy.

Please accept my thanks for all the many acts of kindness that I have received in your home and be assured that,

I am,

Yours most sincerely,

....

Ⅳ.未婚夫妻的信件

給未婚夫

（Date）

My dearest Bill,

I am writing this early in order that I may be sure it will reach you in time for Christmas. How different a Christmas it will be for both of us from last one. Just think of next Christmas！We shall both be together then, won't we？I'm sending you a volume of Swinburne's *Poems and Ballads* as a little present. I know you are very fond of him. We both are, indeed. I have written both our names in it, as Recipient and Donor. Do you like it, dear Bill？Do let me know.

I am working you a sweater of your old colours, but I get on so slowly. However, it will be ready for you when you return. I am counting the days till then. How long is it？Two months！you will just be arriving in the spring. How I wish it was then now. That's not much use, is it？

Papa and Mother are very well and send their love. Mother is also sending you a box of smashed date cooked pie. Don't make yourself ill. I've seen it. It looks so indigestible.

Fondest love from,
Babs

* I am writing … Do let me know.

　　我提早寫這封信，是希望你能在聖誕節時就收到。這個聖誕節和上次我倆共渡的那次真有天壤之別，想想，下次的聖誕節我們就可以再在一起了，不是嗎？我要送你一本史文本恩的詩歌集當做禮物，我知道你很喜歡他。事實上，我們都喜歡他。我把我們的名字都寫在上面，一個接受者一個贈予者，親愛的比爾，你喜歡這樣嗎？來信告訴我。

* Swinburne 〔'swɪnbən〕史文本恩（A.C. Swinburne 1837—1909 英國詩人及批評家）

* recipient and donor 接受者與贈予者

* smashed date cooked pie 棗泥酥餅

* indigestible 〔͵ɪndə'dʒɛstəbḷ〕 *adj.* 難消化的

回未婚妻

（Date）

My own darling Babs,

Your letter reached me in good time for Christmas, as also did the smashed date cooked pie your mother sent me. I have written to thank her. And thank you a thousand times for *Poems and Ballads*. It has always been a favourite of mine, but now it will be forever doubly dear. I thought of you all Christmas day, and wondered what you were doing and whether you were thinking of me. I remember our last Christmas. It seems only like yesterday. It is hard to think of Taipei's wintry weather. It's warmer here. I am looking forward to that sweater. How sweet of you to work it for me! I hope you got my letter in time and the little present. I had one day's holiday at Christmas. I spent them on the Wuling Farm. I ate such a lot of fruit. I expect you all spent your Christmas indoors because it's so cold. How gladly I would have exchanged all our sunshine just to have been with you. I will be home in February. Just think of that!

Always your loving,

Bill

---

* *in good time* 適時；不誤時
* ballad〔'bæləd〕*n.* 民謠；民歌
* wintry〔'wɪntrɪ〕*adj.* 寒冷的；如冬的

給未婚妻

(Date)

My darling Chris,

I am writing this line to reach you first thing on your birthday, tomorrow morning. Many, many happy returns of the day, dearest Chris. When your next birthday comes round, I hope I shall not have to write you my good wishes! I am sending you a little brooch which I chose yesterday, and which I think you will like. I got it at the same shop where we chose the ring, and I think the man guessed who it was for, as I saw him smiling. Of course I will come round on Sunday as usual, but I thought I would just write this note to send you my love specially for your birthday.

Your ever devoted,
Gene

* brooch 〔brotʃ, brutʃ〕*n.* 女用胸針；領針

回未婚夫

（Date）

My darling Gene,

　　It was delightful of you to write me such a dear letter for my birthday, and to send me such a beautiful brooch. I shall treasure them both as long as I live. Fancy being twenty-four! It seems very old. I keep saying to myself "By the time you are twenty-five you will have changed your name!" It makes me feel so staid! Come early on Sunday. We will go on a long walk in the afternoon.

Much love from,

Chris

---

* staid〔sted〕*adj.* 踏實的；沉著的

V. 夫妻間的信件

給 妻 子

（Date）

My own dear girl,

Only six more towns to visit, darling, and I will be on my way home. However, it will seem a dozen years before I get through them. I just can't wait to be back with you and Lucy.

I visited with the Dicksons yesterday. You remember Victor Dickson — we had him for dinner when he was in Taipei last year. He signed a new three-year contract, which makes the trip a bang-up success. I have already filled up my quota for the month, and I still have a dozen good customers to see.

It will be great to be home again! Even the best hotel seems desolate without your adorable presence.

You'll be delighted with a little gift I picked up for you yesterday. I know how you love surprises, so I won't even give you a hint as to what it is.

Love and kisses from

Your devoted husband,

....

* ***bang-up***　（美俚）上等的；一流的
* quota〔'kwotə〕*n.* 配額；限額
* desolate〔'dɛslɪt〕*adj.* 荒涼的；孤獨的

給丈夫

(Date)

Jeff dear,

You are the most wonderful husband in the world! Your letter was waiting for me when I got back from marketing, and it was like sudden sunshine on a cloudy day. If you were here this minute, I'd hug you to pieces.

Time seems to just creep by when you're gone. And although I'm proud as Punch of the success you are having, I'm still counting the minutes till you come home.

Everything here is fine. The new television set arrived, and it works perfectly. Jack helped me put it near the sofa, where you wanted it. You were absolutely right — the screen is visible from every part of the room. My, what a smart husband I have! Jack looks wonderful, thanks to your sister's cooking. Marriage has really made a new man of him.

You're not the only one with a surprise. Wait till you get home and take a peek into your study! I won't say any more, but I'm sure you will like what you see there.

Good night, my dearest. Dream of me as I will of you, and wake up in the morning with the happy thought that we are one day closer to seeing each other again.

Lovingly,

....

* You are the most wonderful husband ⋯ till you come home.

　　你眞是世界上最好的丈夫，你的信躺在信箱中等我，直到我從市場回來，就像陰天裡突然出現的陽光，如果你在這裡，我一定要緊緊的擁抱你。

　　你走後，時間不知不覺地溜走，雖然我爲你的成就感到驕傲，但我仍數著日子等你，寧可你早回來。

* hug〔hʌg〕vt. 緊抱；摟抱

* creep by　（時間）不知不覺地消失

* (as) *proud as Punch*　神氣十足的

* peek〔pik〕vi. 偸看；窺見

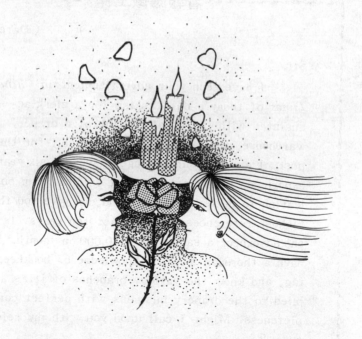

第十章　工作類

　　近年來，由於工商業的發展，對外貿易也增加，因此，使用英文求職信的機會很多；如果能夠寫得好，表達得夠清楚詳細，將能使雇主了解你的能力、資格，而且留下深刻的印象，有助於你掌握此職位。

Ⅰ.找工作

1.看報應徵

───── 看報應徵工作 ─────

(Date)

Sir,

　　I have seen your advertisement in *China Times* of today's date asking for a clerk acquainted with the usual routine of a drapery warehouse, and I wish to offer myself for the post. I am 27 years of age, have had six years' experience in my present post (which I am only leaving to better myself), and can give you the highest references for the last ten years. I should expect a salary of $ 30,000 a month. I have a thorough working knowledge of bookkeeping, and know the various branches of it as applied to the drapery business with perfect completeness. Might I call upon you with my references?

　　　　　　I am
　　　　　　Yours obediently,
　　　　　　..................

＊　　看了您在中國時報所登的廣告，徵衣料、織品零售商店，處理日常事務的熟手，我希望應徵這個工作。我今年 27 歲，目前的工作有六年的經驗，（我離職只是希望求得更好的發展。）而且可以給你過去十年來的介紹信。我的希望待遇是月薪三萬元。我對簿記了解得很透徹，而且了解其相關的知識，有足夠的能力將之運用於衣料、織品業務。我可以帶著介紹信來拜訪您嗎？

＊ drapery〔ˈdrepərɪ〕 *n*. 衣料織品

＊ warehouse〔ˈwɛr͵haʊz〕 *n*. 大的零售商店

＊ bookkeeping〔ˈbʊk͵kipɪŋ〕 *n*. 簿記

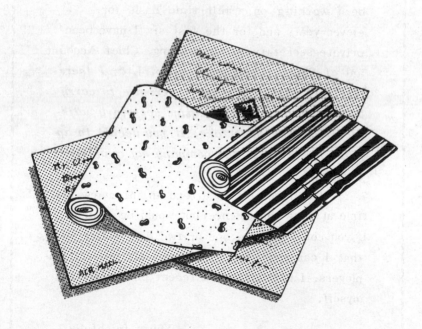

看報應徵工作㈡

（Date）

Dear Sir,

I have seen your advertisement for the post of Executive Secretary that appeared this morning in the *United Daily News* and would like to apply for it.

I have pleasure in enclosing my personal résumé. As you will be able to see, I have been working on a full-time basis for eleven years and for the last six I have been private secretary to Mr. Chuang, Chief Accountant of Philips Electronics Corp. Ltd. *I therefore feel that I have the experience to carry out the duties of an executive secretary satisfactorily, and undertake, if you decide to appoint me, to give the company my complete loyalty.*

I will be able to attend an interview any time at your convenience, but would be grateful if you could give me one or two days' notice so that I can apply for leave from my present employers. I now enclose a recent photograph of myself.

Yours faithfully,

....

Encls.

* I therefore feel that I … my present employers.

　　因此，我覺得我的經驗，足以圓滿的達成執行秘書的職責。而且，我擔保，如果你決定雇用我，我絕對忠於職守。

　　如果我們彼此都方便的話，我隨時可以面談。不過如果您能給我一、兩天時間，讓我向現在的老板提出辭呈，我將很感謝。

* executive secretary　執行秘書

* undertake〔,ʌndə'tek〕*vt*. 擔保；承諾

* appoint〔ə'pɔɪnt〕*vt*. 任命；任用

看報應徵工作㈢

（Date）

Dear Sir,

If an ability to take direction well, and to carry out orders faithfully is important to you, then I may be a good man for the job you advertised in the *Central Daily News* of August 15.

The job sounds particularly interesting because it is precisely the kind of work I have wanted to do for many years. My working experience thus far has, I think, given me the attitudes and the understanding that would enable me to learn the details of the position you've advertised.

I'd very much appreciate the chance to talk to you, and to get your opinion on whether my background and inclinations would be suitable for the job you offer.

I can be reached by telephone at（02）2308-4123.

Sincerely,

....

* If an … for the job. 如果你要的是肯接受指導、且能忠心地執行命令的人，那麼我是最適合於這個工作的人。

看報應徵工作㈣

（Date）

Dear Sir,

　　Your advertisement for a production manager in the June 11 *China Daily News* *interested me because your requirements closely parallel my working experience.*

　　As the enclosed résumé indicates, I've had more than ten years' experience in all phases of production. For the past eight years, I've supervised a work force of at least a dozen people.

　　I'll be happy to tell more about my experience in an interview. You can reach me during the day at（02）2951-2345, and in the evenings at（02）2952-9876.

　　　　　　　　　　　Sincerely,

　　　　　　　　　　　………………

Encls.

---

* Your advertisement for … parallel my working experience.

　　　你徵生產部經理的廣告，讓我覺得很有興趣，因爲你的要求和我的工作經驗很相近。

* production manager　生產部經理

看報應徵工作㈤

(Date)

Dear Sir,

I am writing in response to your advertisement in this morning's newspaper. I am quite interested in the job you have to offer in your typing department.

I am 26 years old, and am a graduate of Soochow University where I majored in English Literature. Since graduating in 2000, I have held several jobs as a secretary in trade companies. Over the years, I have become quite experienced as a typist. I have done both business letters and reports.

At the present time, I am looking for a new and challenging job. Your advertisement indicated to me that the job opening in your company is exactly what I am looking for.

In that regard, I hope that you will give my application due consideration. If required, you may check with my previous employers, who I am sure will be glad to tell you about my personality and work habits.

If I can supply you with any other needed information about myself, please don't hesitate to let me know.

Thank you for your cooperation. I hope to hear from you soon！

Sincerely,

....

* 我要應徵貴公司今天早上報紙所登的徵人廣告，我對貴公司打字部的工作很感興趣。

我今年二十六歲，是東吳大學畢業，主修英文。自從 2000 年畢業以來，我在幾家貿易公司做過秘書工作。這幾年來，我打字已很熟練了。我處理商業書信並做過報告。

目前、我在找一個新而富挑戰性的工作，由貴公司所登廣告中，可看出這個工作正是我所要找的。

關於這點，希望貴公司能仔細加以考慮。如果有需要的話，請向我以前的老板查詢一下，相信他會很樂意告訴貴公司，我的人格和工作習慣。

如果需要我提供任何關於我本身的資料，請不要猶豫，立刻告訴我。

謝謝您的合作，希望很快能收到貴公司的回音！

* *at the present time* 目前

看報應徵工作㈥

（Date）

Dear Sir,

I have seen your advertisement for the post of female clerk that appeared today in the *China Post* and wish to apply for it.

I have pleasure in enclosing my personal résumé. As you will be able to see from this, **I have had some experience of import/export documentation and in typing.** I believe that my present employers are satisfied with my work and the only reason why I wish to leave them is that **I am anxious to widen my experience and work for a larger company where I hope I will have better prospects.**

I will be able to attend an interview at any time, but would be grateful if you could give me two days' notice so that I can apply for leave from my present employers. I enclose a recent photograph of myself.

I hope to hear from you soon.

Yours faithfully,

....

Encls.

* I have … prospects. 我處理過進、出口文件且會打字。我想目前的老板很滿意我的工作，而我離開他是因我渴望到大的公司開拓經驗及前途。

看報應徵工作㈦

（Date）

Dear Sir,

    The sales job which you describe in your advertisement in the *China Times* of October 7 *is one for which I think I can show you some excellent qualifications.*

    You ask for a "go-getter with proven experience." As you'll see from my résumé, I've turned in an above-average sales record for the past five years, ever since entering the sales field.

    While I'm quite happy in my present work, the description of your job sounds even more appealing. I'd enjoy discussing my qualifications with you at your convenience.

                     Sincerely,

                   ....

Encls.

---

* go-getter 工作認眞的人
* proven〔ˊpruvən〕*adj*. 已證明的

看報應徵工作(八)

（Date）

Dear Sir,

I have seen the advertisement for a junior clerk that you placed in the *China Post* today, October 2nd, and wish to apply for it.

I am nineteen years old and have just left Ming Chuan College where I studied from 2000 till this year.

Since leaving school I have been helping my father in his shop on Lin I Street and now wish to broaden my experience by working for a larger company.

I enclose a testimonial from the Principal of Ming Chuan College.

I am able to attend an interview at any time and, if appointed, can start work on October 2nd. The salary I expect is $ 25,000 to $ 28,000. I enclose a photograph of myself.

Yours faithfully,

....

Encls.

---

* I am nineteen … working for a larger company. 我今年十九歲，二〇〇〇年開始唸銘傳女子專科學校，今年剛畢業。畢業後，我在父親開在臨沂街的店面幫忙，現在希望找家大一點的公司，來增加我的工作經驗。
* testimonial〔͵tɛstə'monɪəl〕 n. 褒揚狀；（成績、品格的）保證書

2. 自我推薦

　　要自我推薦到一家公司，而不能確知他們要什麼樣的人時，履歷表可以選擇各種工作都適用的寫法，也可以只強調最強的能力。但由於每個人都有他覺得最適合他自己，而且願意去從事的工作，因此，最好是選擇後者。

自我推薦

（Date）

Dear Mr. Jackson,

　　Having watched your company's growth for several years, I've often felt that I'd like to be able to contribute to that growth by becoming a member of your sales force.

　　Your company appears to attract men who are capable of growth, and who are willing to shoulder responsibility, As the enclosed résumé will indicate, my working career has been marked by both characteristics.

　　I think my experience would fit me particularly well for opening new accounts. I'm accustomed to putting in a nine-hour day, plus some homework in the evenings. Hard work doesn't bother me, since I enjoy selling — particularly selling the kinds of products which your company makes.

I'll plan on calling your office on Wednesday, March 6, in the morning, to see whether I might have an interview.

Sincerely,

....

Encls.

---

* Having watched ··· by both characteristics.

幾年來眼看著貴公司的成長，我常想常爲貴公司的一員，以致力於其成長。

貴公司看起來很能吸引，能夠不斷成長，而且願意負擔重任的年輕人。由附上的履歷表，可以看出我有這兩種性格。

自我推薦㈡

（Date）

Gentlemen,

I venture to write to you to find out whether you could offer me any post in your firm as a ledger clerk. I am thirty-four years of age, and have been twelve years in my present position, which I am only leaving owing to the winding up of the business. I could give you the highest references from my present employers. For the last five years I have been in receipt of a salary of $35,000 a month, and this is what I should expect in any future post I might obtain. If you will allow me, I should be glad to give you any further particulars personally, and hand you at the same time my letters of reference. Hoping for a favourable answer,

I remain,

Yours truly,

....

---

* ledger〔ˈlɛdʒɚ〕*n.*（簿記）總帳
* *wind up* 解散（公司）；結束（事業）
* receipt〔rɪˈsit〕*n.* 收款；領收

自我推薦㈢

(Date)

Dear Mr. Wang,

I venture to write to you to ask whether it would be possible for you to give me a job in your office, or, if that is out of the question, an introduction that might enable me to get a job elsewhere. My wish is to start at a very modest salary with the chance of working my way up through my own efforts. I am now eighteen, and I have been seriously considering what I ought to do for my living. If you could in any way give me advice or help I should be only too grateful. My handwriting, as you will see from this letter, is clear and legible, and I have a good knowledge of figures. I feel sure that I would soon be able to learn to make myself useful in business, and even if you cannot do anything for me I trust you will forgive my troubling you with this application.

Yours sincerely,

....

* I venture to … get a job elsewhere.

我斗膽要求您,是否能在您的公司裏,幫我安揷一個職位,如果不可能的話,能否介紹我到別的公司。

3. 如何寫好履歷表

履歷表最重簡明、正確、清晰，盡可能地寫出自己的長處，及你所應徵的這個工作，其主管最希望知道的事，各個項目都要寫，但切記不要為了湊字數而東拉西扯。

(一) 有工作經驗者的履歷表

Wang Hsueh - wen
230 Tai Yuan Road
Taipei
Telephone : (02) 2891-7274

RÉSUMÉ OF WORKING EXPERIENCE

2001—2003　Sales Manager
　　　　　　ABC Electronic Corp.
　　　　　　Taipei
　　　　　　Supervised sales force of 20 men selling radio and
　　　　　　TV components. Responsible for recruitment,
　　　　　　training, and the establishment and fulfillment of
　　　　　　sales goals. During this period , region's sales
　　　　　　rose an average of 30% annually, compared to
　　　　　　previous rise of 18% .

　　　　　　Presently employed by the firm, but family owner-
　　　　　　ship prevents rising any higher in the foreseeable
　　　　　　future.

1997—2001　Field Salesman
　　　　　　DEF Sales & Service Co.
　　　　　　Chungli , Taoyuan
　　　　　　Sold hardware to stores and supermarket chains.
　　　　　　Opened up new territory after six months on job
　　　　　　and built it up to second largest in company.

　　　　　　Left to assume better-paying job with ABC Electronic.

1995—1997　GHI Engineering Co.
　　　　　　Taoyuan

Designed machine tools for the automobile industry. In last six months of work, became a customer engineer. Left in order to became a full-time salesman.

EDUCATION

College :   National Taiwan University, Taipei, Taiwan.
B.S. (Engineering), 1993

High School : Taipei Municipal Chien-Kuo Senior High School, Taipei, Taiwan.

PERSONAL

Age :   35
Married :   1995
Children :   Two, ages 5, 7
Health :   Excellent
Height :   5'9″ Weight : 160
Affiliations : Sales Executives Club of Taipei
Hobbies :   Tennis

SERVICE

1993—1995   Chinese Army.
Enlisted as Platoon leader

REFERENCES

Available

---

* recruitment〔rɪˈkrutmənt〕*n.* 補充;招募
* family ownership 家族企業
* field salesman 市調售貨員(市場調查)
* hardware〔ˈhɑrd‚wɛr〕*n.* (電子計算機的)硬體
* affiliation〔ə‚fɪlɪˈeʃən〕*n.* 入會;加盟
* service〔ˈsɝvɪs〕*n.* 服役;兵役

(二) 剛畢業者的履歷表

Résumé of
Lin Wen - ling
4 F, No. 11, Lane 200
Tung Hwa Street , Taipei
Telephone : (02) 2701-2345

OBJECTIVE

Laboratory Technician

SCHOLASTIC RECORD— COLLECE

1999—2003　Fu Jen Catholic University
　　　　　　　Hsin-Chuang , Taipei
　　　　　　　B. Sc., 2003
　　　　　　　Majored in Biology
　　　　　　　　Scholastic Average : B plus
　　　　　　　Minored in Mathematics
　　　　　　　　Scholastic Average : B plus
　　　　　　　Scholarships :
　　　　　　　　2002 : Retired Serviceman's Dependent Scholarship
Working Experience
2002—2003　Laboratory Assistant , Taiwan Veterans General
　　　　　　　Hospital. Work involved blood , urine analyses ;
　　　　　　　record-keeping. Average 5 hours per week during
　　　　　　　the school year. Worked fulltime during summers
　　　　　　　of 2002 and 2003.
2000—2001　Clerical Assistant , Biology Department , Fu Jen
　　　　　　　Catholic University. Maintained records of ABC
　　　　　　　Foundation project on the body chemistry of
　　　　　　　twins.
Extracurricular activities
2000—2001　Society of Biology ; Treasurer 1999
1999—2003　Women's Tennis Team ; co-captain 2002, 2003
Sorority :　　Honorary Society of Biology Department

SCHOLASTIC RECORD—HIGH SCHOOL

1978 — 1980   Taipei Municipal Chung Shan Girls' Senior High
School
Taipei
   Scholastic Average : A minus
   Scholastic Recognition :
      In 2000, won DEF Science Fair prize for an
      exhibit on the spectroscopic analysis of the
      stars.
Extracurricular activities :
   Tennis Club— 1997—1999
   Orchestra — 1997—1999
   Glee Club— 1997—1998

PERSONAL

〔 Follow model of previous résumé 〕

REFERENCES
Available

---

* Retired Servieeman's Dependent Scholarship 榮民子女獎學金
* urine 〔'jurɪn 〕 *n.* 尿
* treasurer 〔'trɛʒərə 〕 *n.* 會計；財務
* co‑captain 副隊長
* sorority 〔 sə'rɔrətɪ,‑'rɑr‑〕 *n.* 女學生聯誼會
* Honorary Society 榮譽學會
* spectroscopic 〔,spɛktrə'skɑpɪk 〕 *adj.* 光譜分析
* extracurricular activity 課外活動
* glee 〔 gli 〕 *n.* 三部或四部合唱（通常無伴奏）

4. 如何寫推薦函 (Recommendation) 與介紹信 (Reference)

在申請學校或應徵工作時，使用推薦函或介紹信，兩者基本上並沒有差別，但細分起來，介紹信包括介紹人對被介紹人各方面的整體看法，而推薦函則主要著重於推薦某人的能力，較為明確，不過兩者可以交互使用。

求人推薦

(Date)

Dear Sir,

I have the chance of securing a good post
in a firm of export trade, and therefore I
take the liberty of writing to ask you whether
you would give me a letter or recommendation.
I was eight years in your employment, and I
believe I am right in supposing that I gave you
satisfaction in every way. *I should esteem it very*
much if you could see your way to give me
this letter.

I am, Sir,

Yours obediently,

....

---

* 我在一家貿易公司，有獲得一個職位的好機會，因此，我大膽請您幫我寫一封推薦函。在被您任用的八年內，我想我在各方面都能令您滿意，若您能幫我寫這封信，我將感佩在心。

* *take the liberty of* ～ 冒昧～

* *see one's way to* ～ 覺得能做～；認為可以～

答應當推薦人

（Date）

Dear Mr. Chuang,

In reply to your request for a letter of recommendation, I have pleasure in sending the enclosed. I very much hope it may be successful in getting you the post you are seeking. Our relations were always of the most cordial description, and I, for one, was heartily sorry when they terminated.

Yours truly,

....

Encls.

* 應你的要求，我附上一封推薦函。我極希望此信能幫你獲得你想要的那個職位。我們之間的關係是最誠摯的，因此這關係的結束，我衷心的感到遺憾。
* cordial〔ˈkɔrdʒəl〕 *adj*. 眞誠的
* description〔dɪˈskrɪpʃən〕 *n*. 種類
* terminate〔ˈtɝməˌnet〕 *vi*. 結束

推薦函

（Date）

Dear Sir,

In reply to Mr. Chuang's request for a letter of recommendation, I have great pleasure in reporting the following. Mr. Chuang was with me for eight years in the capacity of confidential clerk, and only left me because he wanted to better his position. During the years he was in my service his work was perfectly satisfactory, and our relations were always cordial. Indeed, I was very sorry to lose him. He is strictly honest, a hard worker, and an intelligent man in the best sense of the word.

Sincerely yours,

....

* *in the capacity of* ～　以～資格
* confidential clerk　心腹的職員；最信任的職員
* perfectly〔ˈpɝfɪktlɪ〕*adv.* 全然地
* satisfactory〔͵sætɪsˈfæktərɪ〕*adv.* 令人滿意的
* strictly〔ˈstrɪktlɪ〕*adv.* 嚴格地
* *in ～ sense of the word* 就本字的～意義來說

推薦函 (二)

(Date)

To Whom It May Concern,

　　The bearer of this letter, Louis Chuang, is one of the brightest young men I have known in advertising. He seems well on his way to establishing an high reputation in the advertising field.

　　Mr. Chuang has a very unusual combination of qualities. While he is one of the most brilliant and entertaining writers I know, he is also capable of writing very hard-boiled direct mail stuff, and is a gold mine to whoever employs him.

　　The only reason I have let Chuang go was because our billing has been cut down to such a degree that we can no longer afford to keep him. We let several older and more experienced men leave us before we were willing to dispense with the services of Mr. Chuang.

　　　　　　　　Yours very truly,

　　　　　　　　.......................

---

* bearer〔'bɛrə , 'bærə〕 *n.* 持信人
* hard-boiled 不含偏見的；理智的
* *dispense with* 免除

推 薦 函㈢

（Date）

Dear Mr. Johnson,

　　This is to introduce a friend of mine, Paul Lee, whom I hope you can use in your factory. He is one of the most promising young machine tool draughtsmen I have ever met. I know that you will find him intelligent and reliable.

Sincerely yours,

....

* promising〔'prɑmɪsɪŋ〕*adj.* 有希望的；有前途的
* draughtsman〔'dræftsmən〕*n.* 製圖員

推薦函 (四)

(Date)

Dear Sir,

Emma Yang was employed by the Hua Hsia Fashion Company from June 1997 to January 2003. In that time she held positions of increasing responsibility, progressing from salesgirl to section manager, and finally to assistant buyer of the book department. At all times Miss Yang showed a great aptitude for merchandising. Her campaigns were always executed with great originality and effectiveness. It was with great regret that we accepted her resignation to seek broader opportunities with a larger organization.

....

Merchandising Manager

---

* 楊愛瑪由一九九七年到二○○三年受雇於華夏服飾公司。在此期間，她的工作責任日益增加。由售貨小姐到部門經理，最後到會計部做經手購貨助理。楊小姐顯得很有貿易才能。她執行銷售計劃很有原創性及效率。很遺憾我們必須接受她的辭職，讓她到更大的公司，尋求更廣的發展。

* assistant buyer　經手購貨助理
* book department　會計部門
* originality〔ə͵rɪdʒə'nælətɪ〕*n.* 獨創力；創作力

求人介紹

（ Date ）

Dear Mr. Chen,

 Although it has been several months since I left Wei's, I have not as yet found the type of work I wish to follow as a permanent career.

 In making applications at several places, it has been necessary to present a complete business résumé, including references. Would you be kind enough to let me use your name as a reference when the occasion arises in the future ?

Sincerely,

………

---

* 雖然我離開韋氏公司，已有好幾個月了，我却還沒有找到一個願意終生從事的職業。

 在應徵了幾個工作後，我發現一份包括介紹人的完整的履歷表，是很必要的。如果再有這種情況，能否請你讓我用你的名字當介紹人？

答應當介紹人

（Date ）

Dear Miss Lin,

I shall be pleased to let you use my name as a reference. We found your work more than satisfactory and regretted the circumstances that led you to leave Wei's.

I know that any company you work for will get the same kind of loyalty, intelligence, and efficiency that you displayed during your three years with us. Be assured that I will not hesitate to recommend you to any prospective employer.

The best of luck to you.

Cordially yours,

....

---

* 　我很高興當你的介紹人。你的工作何止令人滿意！很遺憾，環境使你不得不離開韋氏公司。

　我知道你將會為你所工作的公司，貢獻出你的忠誠、智慧和效率，就像你在我們這裡的三年。如果你有有希望的工作，我一定毫不遲疑地幫你寫推薦函。

　祝福你！

求介紹信

（Date）

Dear Sir,

Mr. Lin has given us your name as a reference. We would like to know how you think he would be able to handle a position as copy chief in our small agency.

In confidence we would like to say that we are greatly impressed by Mr. Lin's copy and by his delightful personality. We wish, however, to assure ourselves that he will be able to keep up a good, steady level of work, and direct the work of others.

We would greatly appreciate having this information from you as soon as possible.

Yours sincerely,

....

*　　林先生告訴我們您可以當他的推薦人。我們想知道一下，您認為他是否有能力在我們的小廣告公司，擔任一名完稿課課長的職務。

我們對林先生的完稿能力和愉快的個性印象很深刻。然而，我們希望確定一下，是否他工作情況能保持好而穩定，且能管理別人的工作。

若能儘快知道您的意見，將不勝感激。

介 紹 信

（Date）

Dear Sir,

Thank you for your letter about Mr. Lin. We agree with you that he is a delightful person and that his copy has plenty of sparkle.

While we did not find him quite stable enough to suit our needs, it is possible that he will show more maturity in a more responsible position. We hope you can give him a trial.

Yours truly,

....

* 謝謝您關於林先生的來信。我們也覺得他的性格很討人喜歡，而且他的手稿也非常可圈可點。

然而我們覺得，就穩重這一點來說，他不太合我們的要求，可能在一個責任較重的職位上，他看起來會更成熟。希望您能給他一次機會。

* sparkle〔′sparkl̩〕*n.* 火花；閃耀

求 介 紹 信 (二)

（Date）

Dear Mr. Ho,

　　Miss Anny Wang has given your name as a business reference. I am considering hiring her as my secretary, and I need a young woman who, besides proficiency in secretarial skills, has the ability to get along with others and work well without supervision.

　　Any information you care to give will, of course, be held in the strictest confidence. Thank you.

　　　　　　　　　　　　Very truly yours,

　　　　　　　　　　　　....................

* 　　王安妮小姐把您的大名給我們，做工作的推薦人。我想雇她當我的秘書，而我理想的秘書人選是，除了精通秘書工作，還需能和同事和睦相處，且不須督促就能把工作做得很好。
　　當然您所給的任何資料，我們都將保持機密。
* proficiency〔prəˈfɪʃənsɪ〕 *n.* 熟練；精通
* *get along with*～　與～相處
* *in confidence*　當作秘密

介紹信 (二)

(Date)

Dear Mr. Anderson,

I am happy to have the opportunity of answering your letter about Anny Wang. She is a rare find as a secretary; a young lady who is accurate, intelligent, and personable.

Miss Wang came to us about five years ago as a graduate of Ming Chuan College of Commerce for Girls. She moved from one department to another as the work required, accepting added responsibilities with cheerfulness, efficiency, and dependability. When she left us a year ago to get married, she was secretary to the president of the company. We were sincerely sorry to see her leave.

Yours truly,
....

---

* 　　很高興有機會來答覆您，王安妮小姐的事。她聰明、做事正確又漂亮，是難得一見的秘書。

　　王小姐五年前由銘傳女子專科學校畢業，來到我們公司。若基於工作需要，被調到另外的部門，她都能獨立、有效率而愉快地承擔額外的任務。一年前她結婚而離開本公司時，是本公司總經理的秘書。我們對她的離開感到惋惜。

* personable 〔ˈpɜ˞snəbl̩, ˈpɜ˞snə-〕 *adj*. 貌美的；儀表非凡的

求介紹信 ㈢

(Date)

Dear Mr. Wu,

Mr. Sung has applied for a job with our firm. He has given your name as a business and personal reference, saying that he has known you for three years and has been your private secretary for one year.

We would greatly appreciate a statement from you about his personality, reliability, adaptability, etc. We will, of course, consider your reply strictly confidential.

Yours sincerely,

....

---

* 宋先生來應徵本公司的工作，他給我們您的大名，做業務和人事推薦。說他認識您已三年，而且當過您的秘書一年。

若能知道您對他的人格、可靠性、適應力等等的看法，將不勝感激。當然我們會把您的答覆視為機密。

* adaptability〔ə,dæptə'bɪlətɪ〕 *n.* 適應性

介 紹 信 ㈢

（Date）

Dear Sir,

　　Frankly I was surprised that Mr. Sung gave my name as a reference. He was with us for only three weeks, during which time we found his work quite clearly below our expectations and needs. He showed little interest in what he was asked to do and, as a result, it often had to be redone. After the three weeks, we felt obliged to let him go.

　　　　　　　　Yours truly,

　　　　　　　　...............

*　　　坦白說，我很驚訝宋先生會把我當他的推薦人。他在我們這裡只待了三個星期，在這段期間，我們很清楚地發現，他的工作遠不如我們所預期和需要的。對於我們要他做的工作，他顯得很沒興趣，以至於後來必須重做。經過三個星期後，我們覺得不得不讓他走。

* *oblige to*～　不得不～

5. 約定面談（interview）

⑴ 資格符合，約定面談時間

約定面談

(Date)

Dear Mr. Chu,

　　Our custom is to have applicants for jobs see our personnel director, Mr. Liu, before they are interviewed by the head of the bookkeeping department. However, we are so much interested in what you have to say about yourself that Mr. Wei would like to see you right away.

　　He will phone you for an interview sometime tomorrow evening.

Yours truly,

…………

* 　　依本公司的慣例，應徵工作者在見本公司會計部門的主任之前，應先見我們的人事主管林先生，然而由於我們對你所說的資歷很感興趣，因此魏先生希望立刻見你。

　　他將在明晚打電話給你，和你約定面談時間。

* personnel director　人事主管

* bookkeeping department　會計部門

約定面談㈡

(Date)

Dear Jim,

In reply to your letter of June 16, I think it quite possible that I might be able to find an opening for you in this company Could you come and have lunch with me here next Tuesday at 1:30, when we can discuss the matter in detail? Of course it would depend on yourself entirely how far you move up in this firm, but at any rate I think I can give you the chance.

Yours sincerely,

....

* 回覆你六月十六日的來信，我想我可以在這個公司裏幫你安排一個工作。你能不能在下星期二，中午一點半過來和我共進午餐，那時我們再詳談細節。當然你在公司的升遷，必須完全靠你自己，不過，無論如何，我想我是可以給你這個機會的。
* *in detail* 詳細地
* *move up* 升遷
* *at any rate* 無論如何

約定面談㈢

（ Date ）

Dear Sir,

     In reply to your application in answer to our advertisement in Economic Daily News, I should be pleased to see you here at 10:30 tomorrow morning. If you are able to satisfy me in every way of your capability, and if your references are all that you say they are, I have no doubt that we can arrange matters to our mutual advantage.

Yours truly,

....

*   回覆你應徵本公司在經濟日報上所登的求才廣告，明天早上十點半，我很樂意在本公司見你。如果你的各方面才能合我的需要，且你的推薦函果如你所說的，那我將毫不遲疑地，依我們的共同利益，來安排一切有關事項。

* mutual〔'mjutʃʊəl〕 adj. 共同的

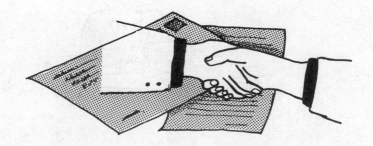

約定面談㈣

（Date）

Dear Mr. Wu,

　　We were very much interested in your letter to us applying for a copywriting position.

　　Can you come in for an interview on Saturday morning at nine o'clock?

　　　　　　　　　　　Yours very truly,

　　　　　　　　　　　....................

* 　　對於你應徵本公司的文字撰稿的工作，我們很感興趣。

　　你能在星期六早上九點，到此面談嗎？

* copywriting〔ˈkɑpɪˈraɪtɪŋ〕n. 廣告文字撰稿

(2) **資格不合**

資格不合

（Date）

Dear Mr. Wang,

    Thank you for your letter of March 17.
While we are very much interested in your
qualifications, we are afraid that you do not
quite meet with our current needs.

    We thank you for your inquiry.

Very truly yours,

....

  *   謝謝你三月十七日的來信，儘管我們對你的條件很感興趣，不過恐怕你不太符合我們目前的需要。

        謝謝你的詢問。

* qualification〔͵kwɑləfəˈkeʃən〕*n.* 資格；條件

* inquiry〔ɪnˈkwaɪrɪ, ˈɪnkwərɪ〕*n.* 詢問；探問

已有人選

（Date）

Dear Sir,

　　In reply to your application of May 12, I regret that I have already filled the vacancy, and that therefore no object would be served by your calling upon me.

　　　　　　　　　　Yours faithfully,

　　　　　　　　　　·················

* 回覆你五月十二日的應徵，很遺憾，我們這個工作已找到人了，因此沒有空缺可以適合你的要求。

* *call upon* 請求；要求

沒有空缺

（Date ）

Dear Chen,

In reply to your letter of June 10, I am sorry to say that there are no vacancies in this firm at present, nor as far as I know in any firm in which I have any friends who might be of help. But I will keep my ears open and if I hear of anything, I'll let you know. However, I would advise you not to cease your efforts to get a job elsewhere as it is very probable that I might not hear of anything suitable for a long time.

Yours very truly,

....

* 回覆你六月十日的來信，很遺憾必須告訴你，本公司目前沒有任何空缺，就我所知，在所有能幫得上忙的朋友中，他們的公司裏也沒有缺。不過我仍將密切注意，如果有任何消息，我將會通知你。無論如何，我勸你還是要繼續到別處去找工作，因爲，很可能我在很久之內都找不到適合的工作。

* *keep one's ears open* 某人在密切注意

6. 決定聘用

面談合格，決定聘用

（Date）

Dear Miss Chang,

With reference to the interview you had with me on 12th February, I am writing to offer you the position of clerk in the Export Department.

Your starting salary will be $ 25,000 per month for the first six months, during which you will be on probation. *If you are confirmed in your appointment, subject to your manager's recommendation, you will be offered an increased monthly salary.*

Normal office hours are from 8:30 a.m. to 5:30 p.m., Monday to Friday and from 8:30 a.m. to 12:00 a.m. on Saturdays. You may be required to do overtime work in addition to these hours and this will be paid at the normal hourly rate for the first hour after normal working hours and 125%·of the hourly rate thereafter.

You will be entitled to two weeks' annual vacation with pay and after five years' service, this will be increased to three weeks' annual vacation.

This appointment can be terminated with one month's notice in writing by either side.

If these terms are acceptable to you, I shall be pleased to have your confirmation in writing that you will be able to take up your duties here at 8:30 a.m. on 1st March, 2003.

Yours sincerely,

....

Personnel Manager

---

* **on probation** 在試用期間
* office hours 上班時間；辦公時間
* overtime〔'ovɚ,taɪm〕 *adj.* 超出時間的；加班的
* entitle〔ɪn'taɪtl̩〕 *vt.* 使有資格

回覆

（Date）

Dear Mr. Chao,

Thank you for your letter of February 22 offering me the post of Clerk in your Export Department.

I have much pleasure in accepting the appointment in accordance with the conditions stated in your letter and look forward to starting work at 8:30 a.m. on 1st March, 2003.

Yours sincerely,

....

* *in accordance with* 依照；根據

* 謝謝你二月二十日的來信，提供我你們出口部辦事員的職位。
我很高興按照你信所述的條件，接受這職位，並期待於 2003 年三一日早上八時半開始上班。

Ⅱ.要求加薪

要求加薪

（Date）

Sir,

I have now been in your service for a period of 15 months, and I believe that during that time I have given you satisfaction. When I entered your employ it was on the understanding that my salary should gradually increase till it reached a maximum of $ 30,000. I am now getting $ 27,000. I therefore take the liberty of asking for a raise in my salary, and I trust that you will consider my proposal favourably.

Yours respectfully,

....

* 　我在此職位已待了十五個月了，相信你對我的工作也很滿意。當我進入公司時，談妥的條件是我的薪水將逐漸增加，最多會到三萬元，而我現在是二萬七千元；因此，我冒昧請求您加薪，相信你會贊成我的建議。

* *on the understanding* 在～條件之下

* *take the liberty of* ～ 冒昧～

同意加薪

（Date ）

Dear Mr. Wang,

I have received your letter requesting a raise in your salary, and have pleasure in acceding to your request. I will raise it by $2,000, up to $ 29,000 a month. It gives me pleasure to say that I have found your work quite satisfactory, and that if everything continues in this happy relationship I hope to raise your salary by monthly amounts of $1,000 until the limit of $ 30,000 is reached.

Yours truly,

…………

* 　我已收到你**要**求加薪的信件，也很樂意批准你的要求，我將加兩千元，就是每個月二萬九千元，我很高興，你的工作相當令人滿意。如果我們這種愉快的關係，可以繼續維持下去的話，我會把你的薪水，再加一千到三萬元。

* *accede to* 批准；核准

不同意加薪

(Date)

Dear Mr. Wang,

I regret that I am unable to accede to the request contained in your letter. It is true that there was an arrangement made between us by which your salary was gradually to increase to $ 30,000 , but I must point out to you first that you have not yet been with me a year and a half ; and second, that my business, as you must know, has not been at all in a satisfactory condition for the last year, and that I really do not feel justified in raising your salary.

As far as your work is concerned, I am pleased to say that it has been on the whole quite satisfactory, and if business does improve in the next twelve months and you still choose to stay with me, I shall certainly see if I cannot manage to raise your remuneration by at least $ 2,000 per month as a commencement.

Yours truly,

....

* It is true … as a commencement.

　　我們確實協議過，把你的薪水逐漸加到三萬元；不過我必須提醒你，首先，你跟我的時間還不到一年半；其次，如你所知，過去一年來，我的生意狀況並不很理想，因此，我不認為應當加你薪。

　　至於你的工作，就整體上來說，頗令人滿意，如果明年一年內生意好轉，而你仍願意繼續跟我的話，我再看看能否設法，至少把你的薪水提高兩千元以上。

* **point out**　指出；提醒

* remuneration〔rɪ͵mjunəˋreʃən〕 *n.* 報酬；薪水

* commencement〔kəˋmɛnsmənt〕 *n.* 開始

Ⅲ.離職

辭職

(Date)

Dear Sir,

　　In accordance with my agreement with your firm, I am writing to give you formal notice of the termination of my service with you one month from now. The health of my wife makes it very undesirable that I should live any long in Keelung, and I have accepted a post as clerk to a firm of solicitors in Taipei.

　　In giving you this notice, I should like to thank you for all your past kindness to me, and to say how sorry I am that I feel compelled to take this step. If I alone were concerned I should not think of leaving you.

Yours respectfully,

....

---

* In accordance with … in Taipei.

　　根據我與公司的協定，我正式通知你，從今天起一個月內，我將離職。內人的健康，使得我們不適宜再待在基隆，而我也在台北的一家律師事務所，找到一個職員的工作。

* termination〔͵tɝməˈneʃən〕*n.* 終止；結束
* service〔ˈsɝvɪs〕*n.* 雇用；受雇
* solicitor〔səˈlɪsətɚ〕*n.* 律師

辭退職員

（Date）

Dear Mr. Hu,

　　Although I have spoken to you several times about your lax attention to your duties, I have been unable to notice any improvement in your conduct. I have therefore come to the conclusion that I must ask you to leave my service. Will you kindly take this as a formal notice of the termination of our contract as of three months from today, according to the terms of our agreement?

　　　　　　　　　　　　Yours truly,

　　　　　　　　　　　　............

* 　　雖然我曾多次說過，你怠忽職責，但卻不見你有任何改進，因此我決定請你離開我的公司。根據我們的協定，從今天起三個月內，請把本通知視爲正式的契約終止書。

* *come to the conclusion* 下～的結論；做～決定

第十一章　學校類

I.在校的課業問題

請　病　假

（Date）

Dear Miss Wang,

Tommy's absence during the past four days was caused by a cold and fever.

He seems to be all right now.

Sincerely,

....

* 過去四天來，湯米缺課是由於感冒和發燒。

他現在看起來已經好多了。

請事假

(Date)

Dear Miss Wang,

We should like to take Tommy on a trip to visit his grandfather next week.

Although we dislike making him miss school, we have been unable to arrange a different schedule.

If you can give him his assignments in advance, we shall try to make sure that he does them while he's away.

Please call me at 2951-2345 if you foresee any problems.

Sincerely,

....

* 下週我們打算帶著湯米,去探望他祖父。

雖然我們不願意他因此而缺課,但是我們實在無法排定別的時間。

如果你能事先把指定作業交給他,我們可以保證他在這段時間內一定會做完。

若有什麼可以預見的疑難,請打電話 2951-2345 給我。

* foresee〔for'si, fɔr'si〕vt. 預知

澄清不上課的原因

(Date)

Dear Mr. Chang,

I am anxious to clarify the situation which ended with Nick's being sent to the office yesterday. He really was telling the truth when he insisted he was not supposed to take gym. Of course, I know he does try to get out of games because of his poor vision, but yesterday I had written a note asking that you excuse him from gym because he had had a sore throat all weekend. He must have dropped the note on the street when he reached for his bus ticket. He was quite upset about being sent to the office, and I am sure all this was none too pleasant for you either. I am also writing Miss Lin an explanation.

We have sent away for a glasses' shield for him, and when he can wear that in gym class he may be less reluctant to play the games.

I hope to be able to talk to you at school soon to see what else you think we could do here at home to encourage Nick.

Yours sincerely,

. . . .

* I am anxious to … writing Miss Lin an explanation.

　我急於想澄淸，昨天尼克被送到辦公室的這件事。他堅持說他不可以上體育課，並不是在撒謊。當然，我知道他由於視力不好，經常想不去上課。但是昨天我確實寫了一封信，請您准他不必上課，因爲他的喉嚨痛了一整個週末。那張條子可能是他在上學途中，掏車票時弄掉了。他爲了被送到辦公室這事覺得很煩惱，我確信大家也都不好過。我也寫信向林老師解釋了。

* gym〔dʒɪm〕n. 體育課

* *be supposed to*　應該

連繫孩子的導師

(Date)

Dear Mr. Chen,

  As the parents of Jack Chuang, now in his sophomore year, we have been disturbed by his poor academic record during the past four months.

  We should like to make an appointment to discuss your ideas about how we might help Jack.

  Will you call me at 2951-7890 any weekday morning to arrange a time when my husband and I might visit you？

       Sincerely,

       ………

*   身爲莊傑克的父母，我們爲他大二這四個月來，學業成績那麼差，感到很煩惱。

  我們希望和您約個時間，了解一下您的看法，到底我們該怎樣來幫傑克。

  你能否在任何一個週日早上，打電話 2951-7890，和我們約個時間，讓我和外子來拜訪您？

* weekday〔'wik,de〕*n.* （星期日以外的）平日；週日

Ⅱ.申請入學

1. 函索申請表格

函索入學申請表格

(Date)

Dear Sirs,

I should like to apply for admission to your Graduate School in order to pursue a Master's Degree in Electrical Engineering. My intended date of entry is Fall 2003.

In June 2000, I obtained a Bachelor of Engineering Degree from National Taiwan University with a major in Electrical Engineering. My undergraduate record is well above average. After graduation, I served in the military for two years and was then able to put some of my engineering knowledge to good use.

I have already taken the TOEFL and the GRE Aptitude Test, obtaining scores of 560 and 1500 respectively. My financial resources are sufficient to meet all my educational expenses.

Thank you for your cooperation.

Sincerely yours,

....

*　　　我想申請入學貴校研究所，修電機工程碩士學位。我預定二〇〇三年秋入學。

　　　我主修電機工程，二〇〇〇年獲得台大電機工程學士學位。我的大學成績高於平均很多。畢業後，我服役兩年，在軍中並且能善加利用工程知識。

　　　我已考了托福和 GRE，分數分別是 560 分和 1500 分。我的財力足以繳付學費。

　　　謝謝你的合作！

*　*apply for*　申請

*　Master's Degree　碩士學位

*　bachelor〔'bætʃələ〕*n.* 學士學位

*　*put to good use*　善加利用

*　financial resources　財力

函索入學及獎學金申請表格

（Date）

Dear Sirs,

As I am planning to pursue a Master's degree in Physics at your university commencing in Fall of 2003, I would like to ask you to send me the necessary application materials regarding graduate admission and financial support.

About four years ago, I graduated from the Physics Department of National Cheng Kung University, obtaining a B.S. degree. After serving for two years in the military, I then returned to NCKU, taking up the post of teaching assistant.

I have taken all of the three tests which you require. My scores were: TOEFL, 580; GRE Aptitude, 730; GRE Advanced, 940.

Thank you for your kind cooperation.

Sincerely yours,

....

＊ 　由於我計劃入貴校二○○三年秋季班，修物理學碩士，因此我想請您寄給我，關於研究所入學與獎學金的申請資料。

　　四年前，我畢業於國立成功大學，獲得物理學學士學位。服完役後，我回到成大任助教職。

　　我已經考了您所要求的三個測驗，分數是托福 580 分，ＧＲＥ 性向測驗 730 分，ＧＲＥ 專長測驗 940 分。

　　多謝您的合作！

2. 推薦函

企管系教授推薦函

（ Date ）

Dear Sir,

I enthusiastically recommend Mr. Chen Kuo-hua to your graduate Business program, I am familiar with Mr. Chen's academic perform-ance in the Dept. of Business Administration at National Chung Hsing University.

As a student in my International Trade class, which requires competance in English as a prerequisite, Mr. Chen demonstrated his su-perior scholastic capability and potential for further academic work in his chosen field. He is well-prepared and has acquired an extensive foundation in the conduct of international trade.

His admission to your institution will prove rewarding and I have confidence in his abilities. Please let me know should you be interested in further information in regards to his application.

Sincerely,

....

Associate Professor

Dept. of Business

Administration

服務機關主管推薦函

（Date）

Dear Sir,

I have been approached by a Mr. Wang Yao-tzung, presently an economist with the Taiwan Sugar Corporation, who has asked me to recommend him for graduate study at your institution. As I consider him to be very well-qualified, I am very pleased to comply with his request.

In 1999, he joined this Corporation as an Assistant Economist to help determine optimum sugar production levels. As he was very dedicated to his work and efficient, he was promoted to the position of Financial Analyst in 2001. Besides having an unusual ability to supervise our computerized operations, he has also demonstrated a high level of managerial expertise. As a person, he is very cooperative and assiduous.

Without hesitation, I should like to say that I am confident that he possesses the necessary prerequisites to be a successful graduate student at your university.

Sincerely yours,

....

* 　　　我一直和王耀宗先生頗有接觸，王先生目前是臺糖公司的一位經濟學者。他要到貴校攻讀碩士，請我做推薦人；由於我認爲他有足夠資格，因此我同意他的要求。

　　　一九九九年，他以經濟助手身分加入這個公司，來決定最適當的糖生產量。由於他很盡職，工作又有效率，因此二○○一年升爲財政分析。在此除了電腦化作業監督得很出色外，他還顯出高水準的管理才能，究其爲人很合作，也很勤勉。

　　　我毫不猶豫地，認爲他具備貴校所要求，完成碩士學位的必備條件。

* well-qualified　有足夠的資格
* comply〔kəmˈplaɪ〕*vi.* 同意；應允
* dedicate〔ˈdɛdə,ket〕*vt.* 奉獻；致力
* assiduous〔əˈsɪdʒʊəs〕*adj.* 勤勉的；有恆的
* prerequisite〔priˈrɛkwəzɪt〕*n.* 必要條件；必備之事物

會計系主任推薦函

(Date)

Dear Sir,

It is with pleasure that I recommend Miss Lin Wen-Ling to undertake graduate study at your institution and receive financial aid.

An outstanding graduate of Fu Jen Catholic University, Miss Lin majored in Accounting from 1986 to 1999. Miss Lin was tops in her class in the Accounting Dept. Her scholastic performance was excellent, and her participation in other activities was equally notable. Although she was never a student in any of my courses, she often consulted and discussed matters with me as she was the General Secretary for the Fu Jen Accounting Association. Because of her qualifications, I recommended her for membership in the Phi Tau Phi Scholastic Honor Society, and she has since become an outstanding member of the Society.

I strongly recommend Miss Lin and feel she has great potential. I would be most grateful for your consideration of her application.

Very sincerely,
Philip Lai
Finance Manager
First Commercial Bank

經濟研究所教授推薦函

(Date)

Dear Sir,

It is a great pleasure to recommend Miss Huang Chiung-hua to your graduate school for admission and financial assistance.

I have known Miss Huang for two years now as a Master's degree candidate at the Graduate Institute of Economics at National Taiwan University. She was a student in my International Economics and Regional Economics courses, and also audited my class on Monetary Theory.

Miss Huang was an exceptional student in my classes and she has obtained a broad knowledge of her field from outside reading as well.

I feel Miss Huang will be a successful graduate student for she is highly motivated to learn and pursues research work on her own. What's more her command of English is excellent, Miss Huang is a promising young lady and has a pleasant personality.

I would appreciate your careful consideration of her application for admission and assistantship.

Sincerely yours,

....

Professor of Economics

Graduate Institude of Economics

3. 入學

決定入學

（Date）

Dear Mr. Madison,

Thank you for your letter of May 16, telling me that Centerville College has accepted me as an entering student in the 2003 academic year.

It goes without saying that I'm delighted, and that I do expect to attend.

Within the next few days, I shall be sending you the information you requested about my scholarship and about my dormitory needs.

Sincerely,

....

*　謝謝你五月十六日的信，告訴我中央大學決定收我為二〇〇三學年度的學生。

不用說我當然很高興，而且我也想去唸。

幾天之內，我將會奉告，關於我是否申請獎學金和宿舍的事。

婉辭入學

（Date）

Dear Mr. Madison,

Thank you for your letter of May 16, telling me that Centerville College has accepted me as an entering student in the 2003 academic year.

Although I am grateful for your acceptance, I shall be unable to attend Centerville because I have made other plans for my education.

Sincerely,

....

*　　謝謝你五月十六日的來信，告訴我中央大學，決定接受我二〇〇三年學年的入學申請。

　　儘管我很高興你們接受我的申請，但由於我另有讀書計劃，因此無法到中央大學就讀。

請求批准延期報到

（Date）

Dear Sir ,

　　I have to inform you that owing to un-forseen circumstances, I shall be unable to en-roll in person before August 15 as specified on the I-20 form. Instead, I can only expect to arrive towards the end of August.

　　As this will be my first trip to the United States, I hope that you will send someone to meet me at the airport. Thank you very much for your assistance.

　　　　　　　　　　　　Sincerely,

　　　　　　　　　　　　…………

* 　　由於事情發生得太突然，因此我只得通知您，我無法依入學許可證所寫，在八月十五日如期親自去註冊。而可能在八月底到達。
　　由於這是我第一次到美國，希望您能派人到機場接我。非常謝謝您的幫忙。

* I-20 form 美國大學院校入學許可證件（證件上註明開學日期）

請求延期一年註冊並通知改地址

（Date）

Dear Sir,

Due to unforseen circumstances, I shall unfortunately be unable to enroll this coming fall semester. Would you please change my date of entry of Fall 2003, The I-20 form for Fall 2002, which I am returning to you, is enclosed with this letter.

Please forward all further correspondence to my new address which is as follows :

11-4 Lane 200
Tung Hwa Street
Taipei, Taiwan, Republic of China

Many thanks,

Sincerely yours,

....

* 由於事情發生得太突然，很不幸這期的秋季班我無法上。能否請您幫我把入學日期改為二〇〇三年秋天。二〇〇二年的入學許可證，已經隨函寄上，交還給您。

有進一步的消息，請寄到新址：

中華民國臺灣省台北市

通化街 200 巷 11 號 4 樓

謝謝！

連繫指導教授

（Date）

Dear Professor Johnson,

I am very pleased to learn from the Dean of the Graduate School that you will be my advisor during my two years of graduate study at your university commencing Fall 2003. With your help, I am confident of being successful in my studies.

To help me better prepare for future study, I need your advice as to what books on Food and Nutrition I should review. I have already reviewed General Chemistry, Organic Chemistry, Qualitative Chemistry Analysis and Quantitative Chemistry Analysis. Presently, I am in the process of reviewing Biology, Biochemistry and Food Chemistry. I should be very grateful if you would kindly give me your opinions on my preparatory work and also tell me which courses I should take for the M.S. degree.

I look forward to hearing from you.

Sincerely yours,

....

* 很高興地由研究所所長方面得知，您將是我自二〇〇三秋季班開始後，兩年內的研究課程的指導教授。有了您的幫忙，我有自信必能完成我的研究。

　　爲了要事先預習課業，希望您能指導我，關於食品與營養方面，應該看些什麼。我已經複習過普化、有機、定性分析、定量分析，現在正在複習生物、生化和食品化學。如果您能給我一些有關預備上的建議，及告訴我碩士學位需要修什麼課程，我將會很感謝。

* *in the process of ～* 在～中；在～的進行中

Dean of the Graduate School 研究所所長

advisor〔əd'vaɪzɚ〕*n.*（美）指導教授

General Chemistry 普通化學

Organic Chemistry 有機化學

Qualitative Chemistry Analysis 定性化學分析

Quantitative Chemistry Analysis 定量化學分析

biochemistry〔,baɪo'kɛmɪstrɪ〕*n.* 生物化學

第十二章　電報與明信片

1. 電報（Telegram）

由於電報文比較昂貴，寫的時候應簡化，但若因此而意思不通引起誤會，則不免因小失大。所以省略應以不影響意思爲原則。

賀結婚紀念日

WE SALUTE YOU AS YOU REACH THE
GOLDEN MILESTONE OF YOUR LIFE
GOOD HEALTH AND TRUE HAPPINESS
FOR THE NEXT QUARTER OF A CENTURY

賀結婚紀念日(二)

MAY YOU HAVE MANY MORE YEARS
OF HAPPINESS AND HEALTH

賀生日

AFFECTIONATE BIRTHDAY GREETINGS

賀 生 日 (二)

CONGRATULATIONS AND BEST WISHES
FOR EVERYTHING YOUR HEART DE-
SIRES IN THE YEAR AHEAD

賀 生 日 (三)

WANT TO BE AMONG FIRST TO WISH
YOU BOTH EVERY HAPPINESS

賀嬰兒誕生

CONGRATULATIONS MAY YOUR SON
BRING YOU HAPPINESS

賀 訂 婚

DELIGHTED TO HEAR OF ENGAGEMENT
BEST WISHES AND HOPE YOU WILL
HAVE NOTHING BUT JOY AND
HAPPINESS IN YOUR LIFE TOGETHER

賀 結 婚

BEST WISHES FOR EVERY HAPPINESS
LIFE CAN BRING

賀 結 婚㈡

CONGRATULATIONS THE BEST OF
LUCK AND EVER INCREASING
HAPPINESS AS THE YEARS GO BY

賀 畢 業

CONGRATULATIONS MAY YOU FIND AN INTERESTING AND SATISFYING LIFE-WORK IN A WORLD AT PEACE

賀畢業㈡

PLEASE ACCEPT MY HEARTIEST CONGRATULATION AND BEST WISHES FOR YOUR FUTURE SUCCESS

* 請接受我最眞誠的祝賀，謹祝福你一帆風順。

謝 款 待

FROM MY PLANE I ONCE MORE SEND YOU WARM THANKS FOR YOUR WONDERFUL HOSPITALITY

婉辭邀請

REGRET INABILITY TO ATTEND
PLEASE ACCEPT MY GREETINGS AND
GOOD WISHES IN YOUR DELIBERA-
TIONS

賀 退 休

IN YOUR RETIREMENT MAY YOU
ENJOY THE MOST REWARDING YEARS
OF LIFE

弔 唁

GRIEVED TO LEARN OF TRAGIC AND
UNTIMELY DEATH OF LEE GREGORY
YOUR ESTEEMED PRESIDENT OUR
HEARTFELT SYMPATHY TO HIS DE-
VOTED WIFE AND CHILDREN

弔　唁(二)

NO WORDS CAN ADEQUATELY EXPRESS
THE DEPTH OF MY FEELING I HAVE
LOST A DEAR FRIEND

弔　唁(三)

HOPE YOU WILL FIND CONSOLATION
IN THE ADMIRATION LOVE AND
AFFECTION WE ALL FELT FOR YOUR
FATHER DEEPEST SYMPATHY

弔　唁(四)

WISH THERE WERE SOMETHING I
COULD DO OR SAY TO SOFTEN YOUR
GRIEF DEEPEST SYMPATHY TO YOU
AND ALL YOUR FAMILY

弔　唁(五)

LEAVE YOU ONLY PLEASANT MEMO-
RIES OF MOST DEVOTED HUSBAND
FOR THE CHILDRENS SAKE YOU MUST
BE STRONG AND BRAVE AS THEY
LOOK TO YOU FOR GUIDANCE AND
COMFORT

2. 明信片（Post Card）

明信片分爲一般明信片和風景明信片，格式稍有不同：

(1) **一般明信片**：正面爲住址欄。左欄寫寄件人姓名、住址，右欄寫
收件人姓名、住址，右上角貼郵票。

背面則寫通信內容，照一般書信格式。

POST CARD

　　　　　　　　　　　　　　　　　　　　　　　貼郵票

Mr. P. Chan,
206 Queen's Road West,
Hong Kong

Mr. John Lee
No. 11, 4F, Lane 200,
Tung Hwa Street,
Taipei, Taiwan,
R.O.C.

---

1. 寄件人姓名、住址　　2. 收件人姓名、住址

　　　　　　　　　　　　　　　　　（Date）

Dear John,

Everything in Las Vegas has an air of un-
reality. Roulette wheels and slot machines have
flowered where the cactus used to grow.

　　　　　　　　　　　　　Sincerely,

　　　　　　　　　　　　　…………

---

* cactus〔'kæktəs〕*n.* 仙人掌

(2)**風景明信片**：一面爲風景或圖片，另一面則分兩欄，左欄寫通信
內容，右欄寫收件人姓名住址，郵票也是貼在右上
角。

POST CARD | 貼郵票

Dear John,

　　At the doorstep of our
cottage is one of the fin-
est bass fishing lakes in
the country. Tension and
fatigue disappear.

　　　　Sincerely yours,
　　　　...............

Mr. John Lee
No. 11, 4F, Lane 200
Tung Hwa Street
Taipei, Taiwan
R.O.C.

---

(3)**注意事項**：

①明信片空間有限，且內容公開，因此內容要儘量簡單，重要的或
機密的事不能寫；結尾問候語可省略，可縮寫的字就用縮寫。

②通信內容不可佔據收件人姓名、住址的位置。

③如爲航空信，需在左下方寫上 AIR MAIL，並貼上足夠郵資。

明 信 片

Dear Harriet,

Fishing, sailing and water-skiing fill our day. There's a good dance band in the hotel in the evenings. All add up to a most enjoyable vacation. I hope you and Tim are having a fine summer, and keeping well.

Love from Sandy,

....

* water-ski〔'wɔtə,ski,'wɑt-〕vi. 滑水
* band〔bænd〕n. 樂隊

明 信 片 (二)

Dear Dad,

Bronzed by the sun. Full of vigor after a few days in the desert. Wonderful place to unwind.

As ever,

....

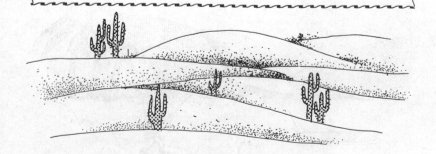

明信片(三)

Dear Mrs. Williams,

It's simply wonderful to breathe this salt air, enjoy wonderful cool evenings and indulge ourselves when it comes to seafood dinners. The Vineyard is all you promised it would be.

Sincerely,

....

明信片(四)

Dear Sue,

Meals any time we choose — no bells to summon us — basket lunches on request — fishing and sailing on the Cape. What fun!

Sincerely yours,

....

第三篇　商業書信

BY AIR MAIL
PAR AVION

第一章 開發推銷類

開 發 信

(Date)

Dear Sirs :

We think you will be interested in a novelty for which we have secured the sole patent rights. The newly invented product definitely satisfies a long-standing want, and it can save both time and inconvenience.

After months of scientific research, a new substance, Texterite, has been developed. The new material is unaffected by water and most chemicals, and it is light in weight without being delicate. Further, it readily lends itself to household uses, as the enclosed catalogue illustrates.

In order to popularize these products, all the catalogue prices are subject to a special discount of 10 per cent during the month of September only. In all probability this offer will not be repeated for some time, and we accordingly look forward to receiving an early reply from you, when we should be pleased to demonstrate the complete range of this novelty.

Yours faithfully,

....

*　　　我們認爲，您必定會對我們得到專利權的新奇產品感到有興趣，這個新發明的產品，必能滿足長久以來的不足，既省時又可免除不便。

　　　經過幾個月來的科學研究才發展出來的這種新產品，它不受水和許多化學藥品的影響，質料輕不易碎，而且，您可由附上的目錄看出，它很適合家庭使用。

　　　爲了使這些產品更普及，目錄上所列的價錢，在九月份都特別打九折。以後不可能再有這種機會，希望您能儘快地答覆，那麼我們就可以給您這些新產品的完整分類。

*　novelty〔'nɑvḷtɪ〕*n.* 新奇物；新鮮物
*　patent〔'petṇt, 'pætṇt〕*n.* 專利；專賣權
*　long‐standing　爲時甚久的；長期間的
*　chemical〔'kɛmɪkḷ〕*n.* 化學藥品
*　discount〔'dɪskaʊnt〕*n.* 折扣

推銷貨物

(Date)

Dear Mr. Johnson：

Thank you for your letter of January 21st, 2003, in which you asked us to send you details of the ladies' and children's shoes that we manufacture.

We have pleasure in enclosing a copy of our illustrated catalogue and price list. As you will be able to see from the catalogue, we produce a large variety of shoes and these are modern in style and popular. We shall also air mail you sample pairs so that you can see for yourselves that they are very well made. The prices that we quote are very competitive, and we shall be pleased to allow you a 5% discount on any order worth more than $250.

We expect all orders to be paid for by Letter of Credit with payment to be made within three weeks of sight and will send you your order within two weeks of receiving your instructions.

We would also like to point out that we have been exporting shoes to the U.S.A. for five years and that all our customers there have been very satisfied with our products.

　　We now look forward to receiving your order.

　　　　　　　　　　　　Yours sincerely,

　　　　　　　　　　　　.................

---

*　　謝謝你二○○三年一月二十一日的來信，信中你提到，要我們送來本廠製造的孩童和婦女用鞋的詳細資料。

　　我們附上一份圖表目錄和價格表，由目錄中，你可以看到我們生產的鞋子很多而且都是最新流行的款式；我們可以以航空郵寄給你幾雙讓你自己看，鞋子確實做得很好。我們的標價是很公道的，如果你訂貨超過美金二百五十元，我們將給你打九五折。

　　我們希望您在見貨三週內，用信用狀付款，我們會在你訂貨二週內把貨運到。

　　我們要指出的一點是，我們外銷到美國已有五年經驗，而且我們的客戶都對我們的產品很滿意。

* competitive〔kəm'petətɪv〕 *adj.* 競爭性的（此指價格比其他商店公道）

* Letter of Credit　信用狀

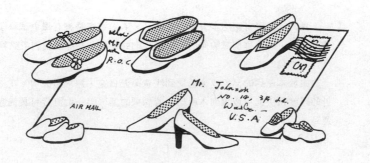

推銷信

(Date)

Dear Sirs:

Have you had an opportunity of testing the sample of our new product we sent you a few weeks ago? We hope so, because every report from those who have tested the samples confirms our claim about the quality.

With the growing awareness of the fine quality of this article, the demand has become very large in these days. Your first order can be delivered within three weeks and stocks will soon be available in your neighbouring countries.

Yours truly,

....

* 我們幾週前寄給您本公司的新產品，不知道您是否有機會試驗了？希望如此，因為每個試驗過的人，給我們的報告，都肯定我們所聲稱的品質。

由於本產品的品質越來越受到注意，近日來，需求量大增。在您鄰近的國度很快就可以買到本產品，若您要的話，第一批訂貨可於三週內運到。

第二章　與客戶建立良好關係類

開戶事宜

（ Date ）

Dear Mr. Anderson：

　　We are happy to welcome your Company as one of our credit customers.　Your account has been opened, but we would like to have some information to complete our records.

　　Will you be good enough to fill out the enclosed form and furnish us with the names of three other firms with whom you do business？

　　We hope the opening of your account will be the beginning of a long and happy association with us.

Very sincerely yours,

....

＊　　歡迎貴公司成為我們的信用客戶，您的帳戶已開了，我們需要更多的資料做好記錄。能否請您填好附上的格式，並提供我們三個和您有生意來往的公司？

　　希望您此次的開戶，是我們長期合作愉快的開端。

＊ furnish〔ˈfɜnɪʃ〕*vt.* 供給

與顧客建立良好關係

(Date)

Dear Sir :

In the daily course of work my attention is directed to many accounts, but seldom to those in good standing. I decided, therefore, to devote some of my time to customers such as you.

Speaking personally as well as for Parker's, I appreciate your consistent promptness in paying your account. You make my work easier and more enjoyable. For that reason I want to sincerely thank you.

If at any time some problem arises in connection with your shopping in our store, please do not hesitate to call on me. I shall be most happy to see that everything possible is done to make your experience at Parker's agreeable.

Cordially yours,

....

* 　 在日常的工作過程中，我的注意力投注於諸多交易中，而未能及於那些長期的好顧客；因此，我決定專注意幾位好顧客，比如您。
　　 就個人和派克公司來說，我都很感謝您付款總是那麼迅速，使我的工作更容易而愉快。為此，再誠摯地謝謝您。

第三章　要求代理類

要求經銷貨物

(Date)

Dear Sirs :

The excellent quality and modern design of your ceramics, a selection of which we saw recently in action here, appeals to us very much. We have since seen your full catalogue and are interested to know whether you have considered the possibilities of the market in this country.

As a leading firm of importers and distributors of many years' standing in this trade, we have an extensive sales organization and a thorough knowledge of the America market. We think your products would sell very well here, and are prepared to do business with you either on a consignment basis or by placing firm orders, if your prices and terms are right.

We are also interested in handling a sole agency for you, which we think would be to our mutual advantage.

Please let us have your views on these proposals. If you are interested in establishing an agency here, our Mr. Eriksen would be pleased to call on you in March, when he will be in Taiwan.

We look forward to your reply.

Yours faithfully

....

* 　　最近在本地活動中看到，貴公司瓷器的精選品，品質優美而且設計新穎，很吸引我們。從那時，我們就看了您全部的目錄，並想知道您是否考慮過，在此地開拓市場的可能性。

　　身為進口業的領導者，且在此行業有多年的配給經驗，我們有大規模的行銷組織，並對美國市場有通盤瞭解。我們認為您的產品可以賣得很好，所以準備和您做生意，只要價錢和項目對的話，寄售或公司訂貨都可以。

我們也有興趣成為您的獨家總代理，我們認為這將是我們共同的利益。

　　請讓我們知道您對這些建議的看法。如果您有興趣在此設立代理商，三月份，本公司伊瑞克先生會到台灣去，屆時將會去拜訪您。

　　敬候回覆。

* ceramics〔səˈræmɪks〕*n.*(*pl.*) 陶器
* distributor〔dɪˈstrɪbjətɚ〕*n.* 商號；配給業者
* extensive〔ɪkˈstɛnsɪv〕*adj.* 大規模的
* consignment〔kənˈsaɪnmənt〕*n.* 託賣；寄售

第四章 訂貨類

詢問物價

（ Date ）

Dear Sirs :

We were informed by Overseas Chinese Commercial Banking Corporation that you are the producer of the captioned products, and would be grateful if you would kindly send us details of your household products.

Please quote for us the prices of the items listed on the enclosed enquiry form, giving your prices c.i.f. Melbourne. Will you please also indicate delivery schedule, terms of payment, and details of discounts for regular purchases and large orders ?

Our annual requirements for household products are considerable, and we may be able to place substantial orders with you if your prices are competitive and your deliveries prompt.

We look forward to receiving your quotation.

Yours faithfully,

....

　* 　　華僑商業銀行通知我們，您製造我們所列的這些產品，因此，能否請您寄來這些家庭用具的詳細資料。

　　　　請依附上的明細表上列的項目，寄來報價單，及保險費算在內，到墨爾本的運費。同時請寫出交貨時間表、付款條件，和定期購買與大批訂貨的折扣詳情。

　　　　我們每年的家庭用具的需求量很大，如果您的價格公道，而交貨快速的話，我們將會大量採購。

　　　　希望能收到您的報價單。

* caption〔ˈkæpʃən〕vt. 附加說明

* quote〔kwot〕vt. 報價；喊價

* enquiry form　詢問明細表

* c.i.f.〔C.I.F.〕cost, insurance, freight 成本、保險費、運費全包括在內的價格

* substantial〔səbˈstænʃəl〕adj. 大量的

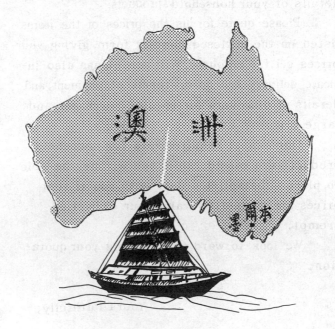

報　價

（Date）

Dear Sirs :

We thank you for your letter of 25 June, and are glad to inform you that all the items listed in your enquiry are in stock. We are enclosing a proforma invoice for the household products you are interested in: if you wish to place a firm order, will you please arrange for settlement of the invoice by draft through your bank, and advise us at the same time.

We can guarantee delivery in Melbourne within 2 weeks of receiving your instructions. If you require the items urgently, we will arrange for them to be sent by air, but this will, of course, entail higher freight charges.

We are enclosing details of our terms of payment, and would be happy to discuss discounts with you if you would kindly let us know how large your orders are likely to be.

We are also enclosing a copy of the report on our household products.

We are looking forward to hearing from you, and assure you that your orders will receive our immediate attention.

Yours faithfully,

....

　　＊　　謝謝您六月二十五日的來信。很高興通知您，您所詢問的項目都有
庫存。我們寄上一張您有興趣的家庭用具的發票形式。如果您是公司訂
貨，希望由您的銀行用匯票付清發票，同時通知我們。

　　我們保證一接到您的訂貨通知，兩星期內貨品就能運到墨爾本。如
果您急著要的話，我們可以安排空運，不過當然這需要更高的運費。

　　我們寄上貨品付款細節，如果您能通知我訂貨量多少，我們很願意
和你討論折扣問題。

　　並附上一份家庭用具說明的影印本。

　　我們期望聽到您的消息，並保證一收到您的訂單就馬上加以處理。

＊ proforma〔proˋfɔrmɑ〕n. 官樣文章；形式
＊ settlement〔ˋsɛtḷmənt〕n. 清償；付清
＊ draft〔dræft〕n. 匯票
＊ advise〔ədˋvaɪz〕vt. 通知
＊ entail〔ɪnˋtel, ɛn-〕vt. 需要；負擔

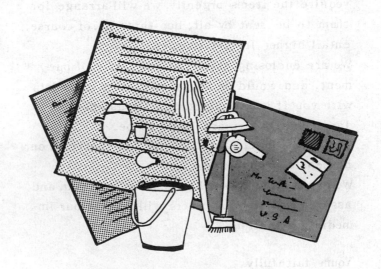

訂　貨

（ Date ）

Dear Sirs :

Thank you for your letter of 12 January and for the details of your plastic ware.

We have now seen samples of your products and are prepared to give them a trial, provided you can guarantee delivery on or before March 1. The enclosed order is placed strictly on this condition, and we reserve the right to cancel and to refuse delivery after this date.

Yours faithfully,

....

* 謝謝您一月十二日來信，寄來塑膠製品的詳細資料。
* 我們已經看到貴公司產品的樣品，假如您能保證在三月一日之前運到，我們準備試用一下。本訂貨單嚴格限於此條件下，超過此日期，我們有權取消訂貨，並拒絕運回。
* provided〔prə'vaɪdɪd〕 *conj.* 假若；倘使
* guarantee〔ˌgærən'ti〕 *n.* 擔保；保證
* place〔ples〕 *vt.* (對商店等) 發出訂貨單；訂購 (貨品)

接受訂貨

（Date）

Dear Sirs：

We are very pleased to have your order and are able to confirm that all the items required are in stock. It is a pleasure to have the opportunity of supplying you and we are quite sure you will be satisfied both with the quality of our goods and our service.

Your choice of method of payment is quite acceptable to us, and we note that this will be by irrevocable letter of credit for a sum not exceeding $500, valid till September 15th. When we receive confirmation of this credit from The Security Pacific International Bank, we will make up your order and await despatch instructions from your agent.

We assure you that this order and all further orders made will have our immediate attention.

Yours faithfully,

....

* We are very … and our service.

很高興收到您的訂單，並且已確定您所要的項目都有存貨。很高興有機會供應貨品給您，我們確信您必會對我們的品質和服務感到滿意。

第五章　討價還價類

要求打折

(Date)

Dear Sirs :

　　We have now had the opportunity to exam-
ine the samples and patterns you sent us on
the 2nd of April.

　　Prices are agreed, with the exception
of the bright style of children's shoes. These
prices are not competitive enough for the market here, and we would therefore ask you to
reduce them on this by 5%.

　　If you agree to this we are prepared to
increase our order to $5,000. Meanwhile we
are enclosing our order for the remainder, and
would ask you to let us have it as soon as
possible.

　　　　　　　　　　　Yours faithfully,

　　　　　　　　　　　...................

---

* 　　我們已檢查過您四月二日送來的樣本和式樣。

　　除了「鮮明類」童鞋外，其他鞋類價格我們不能同意。這些價格在
此地市場沒有足夠的競爭性，因此希望您能減價約百分之五。

　　如果您同意的話，我們的訂貨將達五千美元，同時，我們也附上其
餘各類的訂單，希望您能儘快寄到。

* have the opportunity to～　有機會做～

* remainder〔rɪ'mendɚ〕n. 剩餘

討價還價

(Date)

Dear Sirs:

We are very grateful to you for your indent no. 32 for 10,000 boxes of paper fasteners. To our regret, we are unable to accept your order at the price requested: $ 20 per 1,000. You will find on referring to our previous correspondence (21 June last) that we gave you our lowest price for this quantity as $ 21 per 1,000. Since then, prices have tended to rise rather than fall, and our profit margin does not warrant any concession by way of quantity reduction or discount. We should, of course, be glad to fulfill your order if you will confirm at $ 21 per 1,000, settlement in 30 days.

Yours faithfully,

....

---

* 　很高興接到您編號 23 號，訂購一萬盒紙夾的訂單。
　　很遺憾，我們無法接受您每千個美金二十元的開價。由前一封信，您可以看出來，我們這種品質最低價格是每千個二十一元，從那時起，價格只漲不跌，但我們絕不降低品質來維持應有的利潤。
　　如果你能把價錢提爲每千個二十一元，並在三十天內付清，我們將很高興地把貨送到。

* margin〔ˊmɑrdʒɪn〕 *n.* 盈餘；利潤

* concession〔kənˊsɛʃən〕 *n.* 讓步

第六章　抱怨類

抱怨品質不合

（Date）

Dear Sirs :

We are very sorry to have to inform you that your last delivery is not up to your usual standard. The material seems to be too loosely woven and is inclined to pull out of shape. By separate mail we have sent you a cutting from this material, also one from cloth of an early consignment, so that you can compare the two and see the difference in texture. We have always been able to rely on the high quality of the materials you sent us and we are all the more disappointed in this case because we supplied the cloth to new customers. As we shall have to take it back we must ask you to let us know, without delay, what you can do to help us in getting through this difficulty.

Yours faithfully,

....

* 　很遺憾必須通知您，前一次貨品質不如以前。織得太鬆，且一扯就變形。我們已分別寄出這次和以前的料子，你可以看看質地的不同。

　　我們一直很信任您的品質，但也因此更失望，因為我們已把貨送給新客戶了。由於必須再把貨收回來，因此希望您儘快告訴我們，您將如何幫我們解除這個困境。

貨物與樣品不符

(Date)

Dear Sirs :

Thank you for your delivery of Parisian Suits which we ordered on August 10. However, we wish to invite your attention to the following points.

1. The colors of the cloths are dissimilar to your original samples.

2. The blue belt supplied does not match the suits.

We are returning two of these by separate mail, and would ask you to replace the whole in correct color. Concerning the airfreight, we agree to pay the extra costs for airfreight. However, your costs for packing and insurance must have been lower for air cargo, and we request you to take this fact into consideration and to bear some part of the airfreight charges.

We look forward to your opinion on these matters.

Yours faithfully,

....

* 　謝謝您寄來我們八月十日所訂的巴黎服飾。然而，我們希望您注意一下以下各點：

　　1. 布料顏色與您原先寄來的樣本不符。

　　2. 寄來的藍色腰帶與套裝根本不相稱。

　　我們將分批寄回給您，希望您換回正確的顏色，至於航空運費，我們願意多付。不過，空運的包裝和保險費用一定較低，我們希望您考慮一下這一點，並負擔部分空運費用。

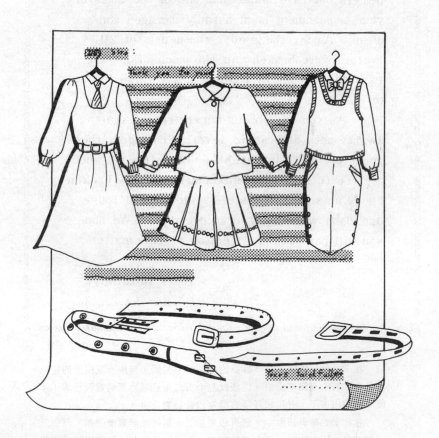

貨物破損，速補寄

(Date)

Dear Sirs :

　　We have received your shipment covering our order No. 281 for 100 units of electric heaters but have found that one of the cases of your consignment is in a badly damaged condition. Among the goods, the panels of 20 heaters were broken and the mechanisms are exposed. It looks as if some heavy cargo fell on it.

　　As you see in our survey report stating twenty sets of heaters severely damaged, these goods are quite unsaleable. Therefore we would ask you to ship the replacement for the broken goods as soon as possible while we will lodge our claim with the insurance company. We hope you will pay special attention to this matter.

　　　　　　　　　　　　Yours faithfully,

　　　　　　　　　　　　.................

---

*　　我們已收到編號二八一訂單的一百個電熱器，但是發現在您的寄售物品中，有一箱嚴重受損。這些貨品中有二十個電熱器的鑲板已壞了，機件都跑出來了。看起來好像有很重的貨物壓上去。

　　在我們的檢查報告中，您可以看到二十組電熱器嚴重受損，這些是不能賣了。因此我們希望您儘快寄來代替品，而我們也將向保險公司提出聲明。希望您特別注意這件事。

* lodge〔lɑdʒ〕*vt.* 提出抗議；訴苦

第七章　催討類

催討貨款

（Date）

Dear Sirs :

　　We have to remind you that the payment for your order No. 283 is due one month from the date of invoice. The order of goods sent to you on August 15 was invoiced on August 16 and payment was due on September 16.

　　Now your settlement is a month overdue and we look forward to receiving your remittance within a week. May we ask you for prompt clearance of all invoiced amount as we have been supplying the goods at special discount subject to payment within a month?

　　　　　　　　　　　　Yours faithfully,

　　　　　　　　　　　　..................

*　　我們必須提醒您，編號二八三訂單的付款期，按發票日期算，已超過一個月時間了。貨物在八月十五日送去，發票日期是八月十六日，付款期是九月十六日。

　　如今您付款期已超過一個月，希望在一週內可以收到您的匯款。我們要求您在一個月內，把我們所寄給您的那些特惠品的所有發票，儘速付清。

* remittance〔rɪˈmɪtn̩s〕n. 匯寄的錢；匯款

催付貸款

（ Date ）

Dear Mr. Johnson :

Your business is sincerely appreciated, and it has been a pleasure to extend you the privilege of a charge account.

Naturally, we do not want anything to happen that will interrupt this relationship.

However, your cooperation is needed in keeping your account within the agreed terms — payment upon receipt of statement.

Won't you please send us your check covering these delinquent items promptly, and thus make it unnecessary to suspend your credit?

We feel sure you will put your check in the mail today, so that you may continue to enjoy use of your charge account.

Sincerely yours,

....

* 誠懇地感謝您這筆生意，我們很樂意給您這個賒款帳戶的機會。

當然我們不希望發生任何事，來打斷我們這種關係。

然而，請您務必合作，在收到借貸表函件時，在協定的期限內付款。

請您立刻寄張支票，把這些拖欠的款項付清，方不至於停止您的信用貸款。

相信您會立刻寄來您的支票，那麼就能繼續享有賒款帳戶。

答應延期付款

（Date）

Dear Sirs :

We have received your letter of June 28 asking us to allow you two more weeks to clear your current statement.

While appreciating your situation, we think it unreasonable to expect us to wait a further two weeks for payment for the goods. Fortunately we are enjoying a good record of settlement and, considering your situation, we are willing to help you as far as possible.

If you will send us a remittance for half the amount of our statement within a week, we can allow you another two weeks for the remaining half. We hope this will be helpful to you and wish you luck in increasing your sales more rapidly.

Yours faithfully,

．．．．．．．．．．．．．．．．．

* 已收到您六月二十八日，向我們要求延後兩週付款的信。

考慮了您的情況，我們認為再多等兩週是不合理的。幸運的是，因您的付款記錄一向不錯，因此考慮了您的情況，我們願意儘可能地幫助您。

若您在一週內能滙來半數款項，那麼其餘的可以又過兩週後再付。我們希望這對您有所幫助，並希望您生意拓展更迅速。

Editorial Staff

- 編著 / 史濟蘭

- 修編 / 謝靜芳

- 校訂 / 劉　毅・蔡琇瑩・石支齊・蔡文華
　　　　張碧紋・林銀姿

- 校閱 / Laura E. Stewart・Andy Swarzman
　　　　Bill Allan

- 封面設計 / 張國光

- 打字 / 黃淑貞・曾怡禎・紀君宜

萬用書信英文

修　　編／謝靜芳
發　行　所／學習出版有限公司　　　☎ (02) 2704-5525
郵 撥 帳 號／0512727-2 學習出版社帳戶
登　記　證／局版台業 2179 號
印　刷　所／裕強彩色印刷有限公司
台 北 門 市／台北市許昌街 10 號 2 F　　☎ (02) 2331-4060・2331-9209
台灣總經銷／紅螞蟻圖書有限公司　　☎ (02) 2795-3656
美國總經銷／Evergreen Book Store　☎ (818) 2813622
本公司網址　www.learnbook.com.tw
電 子 郵 件　learnbook@learnbook.com.tw

> 售價：新台幣二百五十元正

2009 年 6 月 1 日新修訂

ISBN 957-519-584-1